Ciara had been moving her hips to the music but stopped dead in her tracks the moment she saw AJ. The scrawny thirteen-year-old she'd split countless Cherry Cokes with three years before had turned into an Adonis onstage: the sexiest guy she'd ever seen.

Books by Hailey Abbott:

GETTING LOST WITH BOYS

THE SECRETS OF BOYS

THE PERFECT BOY

WAKING UP TO BOYS

The PERFECT BOY

Hailey ABBOTT

HARPER TEEN

An Imprint of HarperCollinsPublishers

HarperTeen is an imprint of HarperCollins Publishers.

The Perfect Boy
Copyright © 2007 by Alloy Entertainment
All rights reserved. Printed in the United States of America.
No part of this book may be used or reproduced in any manner
whatsoever without written permission except in the case
of brief quotations embodied in critical articles and reviews.
For information address HarperCollins Children's Books,
a division of HarperCollins Publishers, 1350 Avenue of the Americas,
New York, NY 10019.
www.harperteen.com

 Produced by Alloy Entertainment
151 West 26th Street, New York, NY 10001

Library of Congress Catalog Card Number: 2006934356
ISBN-10: 0-06-082434-4 — ISBN-13: 978-0-06-082434-1

Typography by Joel Tippie
❖
First Edition, 2007

The Perfect Boy

Chapter One

I don't wanna be a player no more
—Big Pun

Ciara Simmons gripped the back of Dougie Hendrick's neck and pulled him closer as his tongue slid inside her mouth. She closed her eyes and breathed in the mixture of sweat and TAG body spray wafting from his skin as the sun beat down on them through the rear windows of his Hummer, which was parked at the edge of the student parking lot at Westwood Prep.

Ciara's mind traced over the past half hour: Dougie had strolled up as she finished cleaning out her locker, shoving a year's worth of old loose-leaf and worn manila folders into a trash bag and carefully taking down the photos of her and her best friend, Em, rocking out at the Black Eyed Peas show and partying on their class trip to Baja. Star of the lacrosse team and headed for USC, Dougie was a hulking blond senior with a small sun tattoo on the right side of his wide, tan neck. Girls loved him, and Ciara had been making eyes at him from across the room in her Eastern Religions elective for the better part of the semester.

As he approached her locker, Ciara waited for the familiar surge of power and excitement she always got when she was about to "land" a guy. She waited through Dougie telling her that she looked good and that he was sorry he didn't get to know her better while he was still at Westwood. He asked if she wanted to check out the sound system in his new Hummer. As soon as his gaze fluttered from her long, dark legs to her twinkling Hershey-colored eyes, she knew that Dougie wanted to touch her. She waited for this to feel good and right, like it always did. And now, in the hot backseat of the Hummer, with Dougie's arms around her and his tongue halfway down her throat, Ciara was still waiting.

Ever since her first kiss behind the toolshed at the far end of the soccer field in the sixth grade, Ciara loved smooching boys. She loved the way they smelled, loved the curious, longing way their lips moved, loved the way they looked like they would do anything to keep kissing her once she pulled away. She considered herself kind of a player—she liked having guys around, but once the initial rush of that first heady kiss wore off, she tended to get bored. And lately, the boredom was setting in faster and the rush took longer to kick in. Ciara had always prided herself on thinking more like a guy than most of the guys she knew, but lately it seemed like every guy she made out with was getting more out of the experience than she was.

Dougie's fingers, broad and callused from so many hours cradling the lacrosse stick, began to creep under the soft cotton of her lavender Miss Sixty T-shirt. Ciara pulled back, clamping her hand over his through the material.

"Uh-uh," she warned him.

"No?" Dougie flashed the wide, open grin that had probably worked many times on other girls. But she was already tired of his smile and his need. She was ready to be out of there.

"Sorry, I don't play that way," Ciara said, removing his hand and scooting away from him on the seat. She stretched her arms over her head, then checked the small gold Seiko watch she always wore on her left wrist. "In fact, I should get going. I gotta start packing."

"Oh. Well, uh, where are you off to?" Dougie asked. He sounded disappointed. She could hardly blame him—he probably thought he was going to score a goal, and she was already calling game over.

"Santa Barbara," Ciara said. "My dad's got a place near the beach." There was no reason for Dougie to know her dad had been living in their summer house permanently ever since her parents split up right after Christmas. That was the kind of thing you only told best friends, not casual hookups.

"You gonna be away all summer?" Dougie asked, reaching for her again. The heat inside the car had plastered his blond hair against his forehead with sweat, and his eyes looked puffy in the harsh sunlight. To Ciara, he suddenly didn't look nearly as good as he had standing by her locker in the hallway half an hour before.

"Maybe." She shrugged halfheartedly. "Maybe not. We'll see."

"Well, how 'bout giving me your number for when you get back in the fall?"

"Who knows if I'm even coming back," Ciara said saucily. She had already grabbed her backpack and opened the door. She hopped out of the car and strode across the parking lot to her cherry-red Jetta. As she slid into the driver's seat, her shoulders began to slump. The high she usually got from landing a guy had never materialized, and the faint scent of TAG body spray in her hair was so cloying it turned her stomach. She couldn't wait to get home and take a shower—even though it would take her thick, kinky hair hours to dry.

Her cell rang as she clicked her seat belt into place.

"Where were you?" Em's voice came floating through the earpiece. "We waited for you after school, but you never showed. We're still on for movie night, aren't we?"

Ciara groaned to herself. Movie night used to be her favorite thing in the world: her and Em sharing vats of kettle corn and mooning over Heath Ledger's sexy accent until the wee hours. But ever since Em had gotten together with her boyfriend, Tim, right before Valentine's Day, movie night had become a three-person affair with guns and car chases infiltrating the mix.

"I had some stuff to take care of," Ciara said quietly.

"Oh?" She could hear the skepticism in Em's voice. "Like what? And does this have anything to do with Dougie Hendrick chatting you up at your locker?"

"I guess." Ciara sighed. She felt too beat to lie, and Em would eventually worm the truth out of her anyway.

"I see." Ciara visualized Em's lips pressing together to form a flat, disapproving line. "And let me guess—the two of you ended up in his Hummer? He wanted to 'show you his new stereo'?"

A strong flash of nostalgia for the old Em swept through her. Before she got together with Tim, Em was just like Ciara—they even used to compete to see who could lock lips with the most hotties. But now that she was lost in the world of domestic bliss, Em had begun to disapprove of Ciara's playerly ways.

"So are you going to see Dougie again?" Em continued. Ciara could tell from the tone of her voice that Em already knew the answer. She frowned as she pulled to a stop at a traffic light on La Brea and Melrose.

"I don't think so," Ciara said. "You know my style."

"Love 'em and leave 'em." Em sighed. "I know. Look, don't you think it's time you maybe chilled out a little on that? It wouldn't kill you to get with someone you really cared about for once."

Ciara frowned. It seemed like Em was more up her butt to stop messing around every day. Ciara had to admit that Tim was a pretty great guy, but that didn't mean Ciara had to go out and find one of her own as well.

Em paused. "You know people have been saying some not-so-nice things about you ever since Lauren walked in on you and Kyle making out at that party in the Valley," she said reluctantly.

"I didn't know they were still together!" Ciara protested. "He told me they broke up."

"Well"—Em sounded hesitant—"that's kind of part of the problem. I mean, when all you do is randomly hook up with people, you don't really know whether you can trust them or not."

Ciara told herself she was just irritated with the traffic on Melrose and not with what Em was telling her. "I know what I'm doing," she assured her friend. "I'm sixteen years old—aren't I allowed to have a little fun?"

Em sighed again. "All I'm saying is that people are starting to talk," she said.

"People can say whatever they want," Ciara snapped, trying to ignore the doubt creeping into her stomach. "But hey, let me go, all right? I'm going to need both hands once I get on the freeway."

"Okay . . . ," Em said. "About tonight. Tim TiVo'd *Godfather* for him and *Save the Last Dance* for us."

"Maybe I'll come," Ciara said. The thought of watching Em and Tim snuggle on the couch all night made her stomach turn. "I'll see how much packing I get done. I want to get an early start tomorrow morning."

"Well, at least call me before you leave," Em said, sounding disappointed.

"I will," Ciara promised, flipping her phone shut and shoving a Lil Jon album into her CD player, hoping the hard, rhythmic music would shove out the bitter taste in her mouth as she battled her way onto the freeway. She tried to pay attention to the beats, but Em's comment about people starting to talk kept fighting for space in her head. She'd always been good about not kissing and telling, but what was the point if the guys decided to talk?

Ciara prided herself on the reputation she'd built at Westwood—as a strong, independent leader who never took crap from anyone. She took all honors classes and was on the swim team, student council, debate club, and diversity committee. She didn't go in for cliques and was nice to everyone, even the nerdy boys who played Warhammer in the back of the cafeteria. If she wanted to blow off a little steam by locking lips with a guy or two, what right did that give people to say not-so-nice things? But now that hooking up left her without the old high-flying feeling she used to get out of it, was there even still a point?

Just the thought of it made the slimy tentacles of regret creep farther into her stomach. Once they reached a certain point, she knew, they would turn from doubt to guilt. She hated the feeling she got that she'd done something wrong after hooking up with a guy, but a few hours after the fact, it always came to sit like a lump of cold, flavorless oatmeal in her gut. It wasn't so much worry over what people might be saying (although knowing there was gossip around wasn't exactly the best feeling in the world either) or whether she'd hurt someone's feelings. More than that, it was the lingering doubt that she might somehow be hurting *herself*, doing some permanent damage that would only become apparent in the future, when all her friends were getting married and she'd find out she was some kind of freak incapable of having a normal relationship.

"You're being stupid," she reprimanded herself as she pulled off the freeway at Santa Monica. "It's the twenty-first century, you're an independent operator, and you like to kiss a boy or two every now and then without a major commitment. It's not like marrying the first guy who comes along is a great idea either. Look at Britney!"

She'd almost rationalized away the lump in her stomach as she pulled into her driveway. Ever since her dad had moved out, the house felt too big for just her and her mom. It was always a faint letdown when she came home and heard her footsteps echo hollowly on the polished marble tiles of the front foyer. When her dad had lived there, his large, booming presence filled the house even when he wasn't home. He seemed to leave pieces of himself everywhere—his shoes in the entryway, his keys on the kitchen table, magazines and papers strewn throughout the living room. Her mom was much neater. Ciara didn't know how she managed to keep the house so clean while working at the ad agency every night until nine or ten, but nothing was ever out of place anymore. Nothing except for Ciara's dad's absence.

There was a note from her mom telling her she'd be at work late (again) and to call for takeout if she got hungry. Ciara sighed. When she was a kid, her mom always found ways to get in family time around her job, like sneaking Ciara on business trips and ordering room service from the fancy hotels they stayed at. But ever since the divorce, her mom had thrown herself into her job to the exclusion of practically everything else. She had always been kind of a workaholic, but in the past few months, she'd spent entire nights at the office, sometimes driving home only to shower and change her clothes. Ciara supposed she got her über-driven nature from her mom, who had fought tooth and nail to climb the competitive ladder of the advertising world ever since moving to LA from Peru as a teenager and marrying Ciara's dad at the age of twenty-two.

Ciara crumpled up the note and lobbed it into the trash before trudging up the stairs to her room. She dragged her suitcase down from the top of her closet and turned on the radio to 100.3 The Beat, her favorite hip-hop station. Ciara loved music that made her get up and move: her iPod was packed to bursting with bouncy hip-hop, from Q-Tip and OutKast to Diddy and 50 Cent, and her dream was to become an entertainment lawyer so she could represent all her favorite stars. The new Beyoncé played as she threw bikinis, sarongs, and flip-flops into her suitcase, trying to concentrate on how great it would be to hit the beaches in Santa Barbara.

But the smell of Dougie's cologne on her hair and the echo of Em's words in her head kept distracting her, and the post-hookup nastiness thudded in her stomach.

She realized that what she was looking forward to most about spending the summer in Santa Barbara wasn't hitting some of the cleanest beaches on the West Coast, but getting away from the mess her life had become in LA. In Santa Barbara, she could get some distance and perspective, maybe get a fresh start. There would be no Dougies trying to lure her into backseats, no Em and Tim lording their couplehood over her, no guys with big mouths telling all their friends about the last time they'd hooked up. In Santa Barbara, she could be whoever she wanted to be. If only she knew who that was . . .

"And now for a trip back to the nineties," said the announcer's voice on the radio as the Beyoncé song faded. "Who's ready for Big Pun?"

The opening chords to "Still Not a Player" came booming through her speakers, and Ciara froze with a lavender bikini in her hand. She hadn't heard that song since she was in middle school. "I don't wanna be a player no more," went the chorus.

"Hey!" Ciara yelled, spinning to address her speakers. "Just what are you trying to imply?"

"Player no more," crooned the background singers.

Ciara knew it was silly, but she couldn't help

wondering if this was some sort of sign that her behavior was getting to be too much. If Big Pun was ready to stop being a player, did that mean she should be, too?

"It's hard to be a player when you're dead like Big Pun," she reminded herself. Just then, the breeze from her open window blew a strand of her hair into her face—and the gross scent of Dougie's TAG with it. The regret returned with full force, squeezing her chest. Maybe, she thought, just maybe she should give this whole random hookup thing a rest.

Chapter Two

Summer, summer, summertime
Time to sit back and unwind
                    —The Fresh Prince and DJ Jazzy Jeff

Ciara loved the trip up US Highway 101 from Los Angeles to Santa Barbara. The road snaked along the coast, coming into kissing contact with the ocean from time to time: the perfect drive to make with your sunroof open and the windows down, singing along to your favorite hip-hop station on a beautiful afternoon in early summer.

It was weird to be making the journey alone, though. When her parents first bought the summer house, they drove there almost every weekend in the spring and fall, her dad blasting old Motown hits and whistling off-key. They always let Ciara sit up front so her mom could have the entire backseat to spread out her files and type away on her laptop.

Ciara spent two great summers at the house before starting high school, hanging out on the beach every day with Heidi, Marlene, Kevin, and AJ, the friends she'd met at the private beach club her parents joined. As the ocean swooped back into view, she lazily wondered if they were still around.

By the time she got to high school, though, Ciara had to say good-bye to her Santa Barbara summers. As a future entertainment lawyer determined to get into an Ivy League college, Ciara packed her weekends with volunteer work and extracurricular activities, leaving no time to head up to the beach house and chill. Forget summers: going into ninth grade, she was a CIT at a day camp for underprivileged children, and the summer after that, she got an internship at Deuter Schlosselman, LLP, one of the top entertainment law firms in LA. She'd meant to at least head up to the house for a weekend but had gotten so busy the time just never materialized.

But this summer would be different, Ciara promised herself. No grueling internships: instead, she would get a part-time job and save money for college while still having time for fun. She would put the difficult, disastrous past few months at Westwood Prep behind her and focus on making friends, checking out great music, and getting a killer tan. Just thinking about it lifted the cloud of stress and misery that had accumulated around her like the dense LA smog. She reminded herself that nobody in Santa Barbara had seen her since she was thirteen. They didn't know about her escapades in upstairs bedrooms at parties or in the backseats of Hummers in the student parking lot. She'd be far away from all of that—and from that big empty house in LA she'd come to feel so lost in lately.

Ciara laughed to herself as she thought of all the lame guys she was leaving behind at Westwood. Maybe they grew them different in Santa Barbara—the fresh air and proximity to the ocean had to be worth something, didn't it? Wind whipped her hair through the open window, and she pictured legions of ripped dudes on surfboards just waiting to show her how deep, broad, and cool the SB dating pool could be.

Perfect town, perfect job, perfect summer, perfect guy . . . Ciara's mind reeled with the possibilities. She could leave behind the mess her life had become in LA and unveil a new Ciara who did everything right. And then . . . well, why go back home at all? Why not just stay in Santa Barbara with her dad and her new, perfect life? She was being handed a chance to change on a silver platter—and she was determined to make it work.

As the miles sped by under the wheels of her Jetta, 100.3 started to get staticky and fade out. Ciara hit browse on the radio, letting it flip past country and Latin stations. A familiar beat caught her ear, and she almost swerved out of her lane when she realized what it was.

Why was "Still Not a Player" on the radio *again*?!

Ciara tried to rationalize that maybe it was Big Pun's birthday or the anniversary of his death or something. Why else would a song from nearly ten years ago be in such heavy rotation? But a nagging voice in her head told her that it was more than a coincidence: it seemed like a sign. She had to admit that she'd been up tossing and turning for much of the night before, and not just in anticipation of the trip to Santa Barbara. Em's statement that people were talking hadn't stopped echoing in her head.

It wasn't so much that she liked cultivating an endless string of random hookups. In a way, she was jealous of Em and Tim's relationship. It might be nice to have someone be there no matter what—someone who could be a best friend as well as a warm body and a pair of lips. It was just that she had never met a guy who seemed worth taking things further than that magical first kiss.

She had always joked with Em that the perfect guy would have to be as driven as herself and hotter than Bow Wow . . . and good luck finding *that* at Westwood Prep!

Still, something about her "love-'em-and-leave-'em" approach wasn't working the way that it used to. With every guy she kissed, the high was shorter and the nasty post-hookup feeling more intense. Now that rumors were starting to follow her around, maybe it was time to stop being a player after all.

The thought made her hands go clammy on the steering wheel. It would be a challenge to change her ways—she was a natural flirt and loved attention. On the other hand, the emptiness she felt afterward was getting harder and harder to bear.

Rounding the bend heading toward Mussel Shoals, Ciara made a vow to herself to curb her hookup habit until she found someone worth taking things farther than the first kiss. This summer, she would either get with the perfect guy or no one at all.

*   *   *

Ciara pulled into the driveway of the simple white house nestled onto a hillside, overlooking the picturesque town of Santa Barbara and the glittering ocean beyond.

Her dad was out the door before she had even fully emerged from the car. "Baby!" he exclaimed, sweeping her into his arms for a huge hug.

"I thought you'd be at work," Ciara said, stepping back to look at him. His strong, dark face and broad shoulders were as powerful as ever, although the divorce seemed to have taken a toll on the skin around his eyes, which was crossed with tiny lines. It had also sent gray streaks through his close-cut, wiry black hair.

"And miss the triumphant return of my only daughter? Never. I came home to make you lunch, but I have to go back to the office this afternoon."

"You're so sweet." Ciara laughed as he helped lug her suitcases from the trunk of her car into the house. Coming home from work to make her lunch was exactly the kind of thoughtful touch her dad had always been a pro at. It often seemed like her parents had a reverse marriage: her mom always off at work while her dad took care of the house and family. It wasn't just their attitudes that were different: her mom was tiny and Peruvian while her dad was tall and black. Even physically, they had always seemed like kind of a mismatched pair.

"I sautéed some crabs," her dad said as Ciara sat at the kitchen table, admiring the cheery blue-and-white-tile counters and the picture window overlooking the bay. "Fresh from the ocean—via the fish market, of course."

"They look delicious." Ciara tore the leg off one and dug inside for the meat.

Her dad sat across from her, beaming. "I'm so glad you decided to come up for the summer," he confessed. His smile faltered. "It's been kind of lonely without you."

Ciara noted the tiny bolt of pain that flitted across his face. "I've missed you too," she said.

"How's your mother?" he asked, not meeting her eyes. She could tell just thinking about his ex-wife was difficult. Ciara knew from listening in on hushed phone conversations between her father and his lawyer in the early stages of the divorce that the marriage had ended because of more than just incompatibility. When her mom started her all-night work sessions, her dad had gotten suspicious that she was doing more with her co-worker Clyde than just drafting ad pitches. It turned out he was right—she had been carrying on a secret affair behind their backs. Even though she'd never admitted to either parent that she knew, Ciara felt like her trust in her mom was totally shaken. Finding out that the beautiful, smart, and ambitious woman she'd looked up to all her life could do something like that to her own family had been overly harsh. That was part of the reason it was such a relief to get up to Santa Barbara and spend the summer with her dad.

"She's fine," Ciara said. "Still busy with work."

Her dad winced, and she wished she'd said even less. There was a moment of uncomfortable silence before he asked Ciara if she had any plans lined up for the summer.

"I was thinking of getting a job," Ciara told him. "You know, learning fiscal responsibility and saving for college and all that. Know of any openings?"

"As a matter of fact"—her dad's eyes twinkled—"I noticed the other day that the café at the beach club is hiring waitstaff. How are you at taking orders?"

"I can always learn." Ciara grinned. She couldn't help thinking it sounded perfect: the beach club café was on a deck overlooking the ocean, so she'd get to breathe fresh sea air all day and maybe even run into some of her old friends. She finished the last of her crab and tossed the empty claw into the large ceramic bowl in the middle of the table. "Guess I'll head down there and look into it right now."

"Don't you even want to unpack first?" Her dad chuckled.

"Unpacking can wait," Ciara said, giving her dad a quick peck on the forehead as she breezed out of the kitchen. "I'm ready for my summer to begin!"

Chapter Three

Dear baby you the picture of perfection
Straight from your million-dollar smile
To my attraction to your complexion

—Tupac

The beach club café looked exactly the way Ciara remembered it from three years before: weathered wooden tables painted white and shaded by enormous green-and-white-striped umbrellas and a tiny seating area inside for rainy days. At three in the afternoon, the place was quiet, only a few of the tables occupied.

The hostess was bent over a fashion magazine spread across her small podium, so Ciara could only see the bright platinum hair on top of her head.

"Excuse me," Ciara said politely. "I'm here to see the manager about applying for a summer job."

The hostess looked up. As soon as their eyes met, both girls started shrieking.

"Heidi!" Ciara squealed as the hostess ran around from behind her podium to give her a hug. "I was hoping I'd see you this summer. I didn't even recognize you with blond hair!"

"Do you like it?" Heidi asked, twirling a strand of her shaggy Ashlee Simpson bob around her finger. "I had it done a couple of days ago."

"It's really cute," Ciara assured her. "Way different than three years ago."

"I know." Heidi wrinkled her nose. "But long and brown gets boring after sixteen years. I decided to go for a whole new look this summer."

"I like it," Ciara said, even though it seemed a little extreme. Heidi had been the picture of conservative, only wearing plain one-piece swimsuits while everyone else paraded around in string bikinis. She was the quiet one in the group, but Ciara had bonded with her over how much they both loved Harry Potter books and taking long walks to the Italian-ice stand at the other end of the beach. Even though she hadn't thought about Heidi much since she'd gone back to LA, she was suddenly overwhelmed with happiness at seeing her again.

Heidi flashed a wide, sunny grin. "So you want to work here this summer?" she asked. "That would be so great. I tried to convince AJ and Kevin to get jobs here too, but they're all busy with this rap group they started."

Ciara remembered AJ and Kevin, the sweet, gawky young guys who formed the male contingent of her beach club posse. She was psyched to hear that they were still around. But . . .

"A *rap* group?" Ciara screeched. "Last time I saw them, they were all into vintage Star Wars memorabilia. I can't exactly picture them sporting bling."

Heidi giggled. "They're actually pretty good," she said. "I mean, I was surprised. You should come check them out tonight—they're playing at this new place in Ventura." Heidi disappeared behind the podium for a moment to rustle around in her bag. She pulled out a flyer photocopied on bright pink poster board and handed it to Ciara.

"The B-Dizzy Crew?" Ciara read.

"That's them. They call it that because AJ says the music is so good it makes you be dizzy."

Ciara laughed. "I'll definitely check it out," she said, carefully placing the flyer in her own bag. "You'll be there?"

"Of course," Heidi said as the doors to the kitchen swung open and the manager emerged. A portly guy in his early thirties, John Carson had limp, pale blond hair and a belly that flopped slightly over his waistband. "How's business?" he called cheerfully to Heidi.

"Just got better!" she replied. "I think we have a new waitress." She introduced Ciara, and John squinted at her through his wire-rimmed glasses.

"You look familiar," he said. "Do you belong to the beach club?"

"Yes, sir," Ciara said, striving to make her voice sound friendly and professional, like the kind of person he would want to hire. "But I haven't been here in two summers. Last year I had an internship, and the year before that I volunteered at a day camp."

John's face lit up, and Ciara smiled inwardly, glad she had managed to impress him. But instead of commenting on her qualifications, he pointed a finger at her and squinted one eye. "Chicken salad on pumpernickel, hold the mayo, Cherry Coke?" he asked, smiling.

Ciara had to laugh. "Yup, that's what I always ordered," she said.

John chuckled. "It was the 'no mayo' that always killed me. You know how much mayo is in chicken salad anyway? Sure, I remember you. You're hired. Can you come in tomorrow at ten so we can start training you for the lunch shift?"

"Absolutely," Ciara said. Even though she was happy

to have the job, she was kind of disappointed that John hadn't asked to see her résumé—she'd created her own format for it on Microsoft Word and printed it out on the ivory marbled résumé stock she found in her dad's home office.

"Great." John reached out to shake her hand. "See you tomorrow, then."

"Right," Ciara said as he retreated back to the kitchen. She turned to Heidi. "And I'll see *you* tonight at the show."

"Yay!" Heidi said. "And then I think there's a house party we can hit afterward."

Ciara left the beach club smiling. In less than an hour, she'd managed to line up a summer job, a hip-hop show (even if it was just dorky AJ and Kevin geeking out on a mike), and a house party. Not a bad start!

* * *

Ciara glanced at the MapQuest directions she'd printed out and swung into a parking lot flanked by garages and warehouses. As she pulled into an empty spot, she watched a shaggy-haired guy in a Green Day shirt zoom along the sidewalk on a skateboard. He leaped the curb and hovered in midair for a moment before crashing down on the asphalt with his legs splayed in two directions, pieces of asphalt flying around him as his board clattered to the ground several feet away. Ciara winced and got out of her car.

She approached the venue, which was marked with a small sign over a large black metal door, and handed the guy at the entrance five dollars. He stamped her hand with a little LEGO guy in green ink. The inside of the building had clearly once been an auto body shop, with hydraulic car lifts converted into booths for sound and lighting and license plates and old gas station signs decorating the walls. OutKast blasted over the sound system, and Ciara was surprised at how full the room was: apparently, the B-Dizzy Crew already had quite a local following. High school girls in tight jeans, slick curls, and hoop earrings stood clustered around the walls, giggling and checking out the scruffy local guys from UCSB in oversized striped T-shirts and dirty Pumas. A group of skinny, dreadlocked boys high-fived each other and crowded around a small digital video camera, whooping over the image on the screen.

Ciara looked around for Heidi and finally spotted her by the bar, sipping a Mountain Dew and wearing the tiniest miniskirt Ciara had ever seen on anyone besides Paris Hilton. As she got closer, she noticed that Heidi had also lined her eyes in heavy black kohl pencil and was wearing a low-cut tank top with a glittery pink kitten on the chest.

Ciara had decided to dress down for the event, sticking with her favorite Diesel jeans and a vintage baseball shirt from some long-defunct team with a ribbed tank top underneath. But next to Heidi, she suddenly felt dowdy. It was almost an exact reversal from three years before, when she'd paraded around the beach club in a series of short, fluttery sarongs while Heidi had only removed her oversized terry cover-ups to dive in the ocean.

"Nice outfit," Ciara said, hiding her surprise at the transformation as she joined Heidi. "Looks like you've really revamped your look."

Heidi nodded. "I'm trying to get in touch with my wild side," she said. "I've been doing the good girl thing for years now—I'm kind of sick of being a little angel. This summer's all about being bad."

Ciara couldn't help thinking how ironic it was that Heidi was trying to do the polar opposite of her. Just when she'd decided it was time to chill out on the naughty behavior, Heidi was going all-out Lindsay Lohan.

"Well, you definitely *look* the part," Ciara assured her. "With an outfit like that, you might get arrested."

Heidi looked concerned. "Not by the fashion police, I hope?"

"Nah—skin is in these days," Ciara assured her. "Besides, it's summer."

"Heck *yeah*, it is!" another female voice chimed in. Ciara turned to see Marlene, another of her old friends from the beach club, coming toward them. A spunky redhead, Marlene was as outspoken as Heidi was quiet and shy, always leading the group on adventures to check out the live squid in the tank at the Korean grocery or break into the abandoned swimming pool at the park. "Ciara Simmons!" Marlene yelled, wrapping her in a hug. "Where've you been all my life?"

"Here to see the ex?" Heidi asked her. Marlene nodded.

"Ex?" Ciara wondered aloud.

"Oh, I guess you were already gone by the time I started dating AJ," Marlene said. "But we got together pretty soon after that, and we just broke up a couple of months ago."

"I'm sorry," Ciara said. She couldn't picture über-nerdy AJ dating anyone, but apparently everything had changed while she was gone.

"It's cool—we're still friends." Marlene shrugged. "But it needed to happen. Plus, I love their music."

Ciara was still deciding whether it would be cool to ask why it needed to happen when the lights dimmed and the canned music faded out.

"Ooh, they're about to go on!" Heidi squealed. "Let's go up front." She grabbed Ciara's hand and began pulling her through the crowd, Marlene following close at their heels. Just as they got to the front of the stage, Kevin came out and took his place at the turntables. Ciara was relieved to see he'd grown several inches taller in the last three years since he once confessed to her that he was afraid of turning into, as he had put it, "your stereotypical short, dorky Asian." He didn't look as dorky either—his shoulders had widened to fill out the loose-fitting Adidas shirt he wore, and he'd traded his glasses for contacts, although his eyes were still partially obscured by a blue visor.

His brow furrowed in concentration as he adjusted some levels on the mixer and then moved to one of the turntables and dropped the needle on the record. A booty-shaking beat came bouncing through the speakers, followed by a vocal line that sounded like it was sampled from an old seventies soul song. Kevin scratched a few times, building the music to a crescendo before AJ leaped onto the stage, landing in the middle of the spotlight and grabbing the mike.

Ciara had been moving her hips to the music but stopped dead in her tracks the moment she saw AJ. The scrawny thirteen-year-old she'd split countless Cherry Cokes with three years before had turned into an Adonis onstage: the sexiest guy she'd ever seen. His face had filled out to accommodate his wide, almond-shaped eyes and long, dark lashes—the ones that earned him the nickname "Flyface." He had on a silver Phat Farm shirt, unbuttoned to reveal the yummiest-looking six-pack in history. His low-slung jeans showed the sinewy muscles cutting into the elastic of his just-barely-visible Calvin Kleins. Forget Bow Wow—AJ had just taken his place in Ciara's mind as the number-one hottest guy in the universe.

What was sexiest about him, though, was his magnetic stage presence. The minute his feet hit the floor, the crowd went wild, hooting and clapping and calling his name. He seemed bigger than the whole room, brighter than the spotlight, more alive than the screaming, sweating masses below him. She couldn't believe this was the same scrawny boy who played lightsaber around the pool with Kevin back in the day. If AJ could transform himself so much, there was definitely hope for her!

Once he opened his mouth and spit quick, complex rhymes straight to the crowd, Ciara finally found her voice and began cheering too.

"Does he write his own rhymes?" Ciara shouted in Heidi's ear to be heard over the music.

"Oh yeah." Heidi nodded. "It's like all he does—when he's not researching record labels. This group is his life. He wants to make it really big in the music industry someday."

As driven as me, and hotter than Bow Wow. Her own

words came rushing back to her as she stared longingly at AJ's glistening pecs and mischievous smile. Had she finally met the perfect guy?

Kevin brought the beat up and Ciara found herself shaking her booty for all she was worth. She could totally picture the B-Dizzy Crew blowing up—they had a great sound, and AJ's looks were made for MTV. She looked up just in time to see AJ reaching a hand out to the audience—straight at her! Without thinking, she stuck out her arm and grabbed it. A current of energy shot through her arm as soon as they touched. Marlene and Heidi's surprised expressions blurred with the bright colored lights around her as AJ pulled her onto the stage.

"You looked great down there," he whispered in her ear, leaning so close that she nearly fainted from his musky smell of sweat, cinnamon Altoids, and aftershave. Be dizzy was right! Her legs felt like Jell-O as she struggled to regain her balance and get back into the groove. Soon, the music and AJ's rhymes took over and she found herself smiling into the blinding stage lights as she danced, throwing in extra moves she made up on the spot.

"Looks like our girl Ciara's back in town!" AJ said into the mike when the song was over. She felt her face flush but took a tiny bow before jumping off the stage and landing between Heidi and Marlene. As the

B-Dizzy Crew launched into another song, she stared up at AJ, thinking she had never wanted anyone so badly in her life. For the first time ever, she knew she had found someone who'd be good for more than just a quick hookup. AJ was everything she'd ever hoped to find in a guy: an amazing emcee who was driven in his career but able to be loyal to the same girl for like two years. He was perfect!

All she had to do now was make him hers.

Chapter Four

We just wanna get you out
To the party everybody's talkin' 'bout
And you don't have to worry 'bout a fee
Ya see it's all vi-a-vi because you're rollin' with me
                                        —Jurassic 5

can't believe how good they are!" Ciara gushed to Marlene and Heidi after the show. They had gathered back by the bar as the venue began to thin out, and she was guzzling an orange Vitamin Water to replenish all the liquid she'd sweat off dancing.

"I told you so," Heidi said. "Definitely not your typical high school rap group. Where are they, anyway? They've been backstage for like half an hour now."

"Probably still taking off their makeup," Marlene joked. "Or maybe polishing their bling."

"Look at all those girls over there waiting to talk to them," Heidi whispered, nodding toward a group of girls hanging out by the stage.

"Groupies," Marlene said, rolling her eyes. "Just what AJ's ego needs."

Heidi ignored her comment and asked if they were coming to the after party, but Marlene shook her head. "I have to get up early tomorrow," she said. "Besides, in between his gloating and girls falling all over him, AJ's impossible to deal with after a show. Oh, I should probably shut up now," she said as AJ reemerged from backstage and came toward them, a huge grin on his face. He nodded at the groupies but didn't slow down. The moment his eyes met hers, Ciara felt her head begin to spin.

"Great show," she told him. She wondered if he could hear the slight tremor in her voice. What had happened to the old Ciara who was always so confident around boys?

"You were amazing!" Heidi chimed in.

"I was pretty on, wasn't I?" AJ laughed.

"So you're an emcee now," Ciara said. "Who knew?"

"Yeah, hey, great to have you back," AJ said. He opened his arms, and Ciara's stomach thumped. She was getting a hug! Wrapping her arms around his broad, strong back sent bolts of excitement zipping through her. There was a raw, animal energy in his embrace that she could have basked in all night—but she forced herself to let go.

"Hey, everyone," Kevin said, struggling up to the group with a case of records in each hand. "Are we hitting that house party or what?"

"I'm down." Heidi grinned, her eyes glittering. "Where's it at again?"

"D-John's place," Kevin informed the group. "He's got a pool and hot tub—*and* his parents are up in Tahoe for the weekend."

"Sounds good," AJ said. He turned to Ciara. "You coming?"

"I'd love to," Ciara purred. She couldn't think of a better way to spend the evening.

"I have to bail," Marlene said. "I need my beauty sleep."

"Bummer," Heidi sympathized, but she was still smiling. She didn't actually look bummed at all.

"You sure?" AJ asked. "You could always come for a little while and cut out early."

"Positive." Marlene nodded, her lips set in a tight line. "But you kids have fun. I'll catch you another time."

The five of them headed toward the parking lot, Kevin straggling behind under the weight of his record cases. Even though every fiber in Ciara's being wanted to walk ahead and talk to AJ, she forced herself to fall into step with Kevin—she didn't want to look desperate.

"That's a lot of records," Ciara said, eyeing the cases.

"Yeah, well." Kevin grinned. "I figured I'd spin a set tonight at the party if I can get D-John's turntables rigged up. It's almost more fun when I don't have someone rhyming over my beats."

"You're pretty competent with those things," Ciara commented.

"Practice." Kevin set down one of the cases in front of a blue Acura and fumbled in his pocket for his car keys. "Hours of hanging out alone in my room train-wrecking until I got it right."

"Sounds lonely," Ciara said.

"Nah, it's great. Me and the music—just the way I like it." Kevin hefted the cases into his trunk, his biceps straining under his shirt. He had obviously bulked up a bit since she had last seen him—Ciara wondered if he'd started working out. "We're going to caravan outta here, so just follow one of us, okay?"

"Gotcha." Ciara turned and headed for her car. "See you there!"

* * *

Ciara could hear strains of reggaeton booming from the backyard of D-John's place as their caravan pulled up the long, curving driveway. A massive colonial-style mini-mansion set into a hillside high above Santa Barbara, the place seemed built for parties, with a large kidney-shaped pool, matching hot tub, grounds sprinkled with flower gardens and gazebos, and an outdoor bar and grill. Kevin went to talk to their host about setting up turntables and Ciara surveyed the scene, smiling to herself as she took in the group of girls dancing together on the deck, the cluster of guys sipping Coronas by the grill, and the couple making out in the hot tub. She was about to suggest they hit the dance floor when Heidi came bouncing up to them, her eyes sparkling with excitement.

"Oh, super, a pool!" she squealed, bending to take off her shoes. "I've been dying for a swim all night."

Ciara watched in astonishment as Heidi peeled off her tank top and miniskirt to reveal a skimpy black camisole and matching boy-cut panties. She ran for the pool and jumped in, then surfaced a moment later, spluttering and giggling. "Hey, AJ!" she called, swimming to the edge and looking up at him with pleading doe eyes. "Come join me?"

"Uh . . . okay," AJ said, shrugging at Ciara. He unbuttoned his shirt and paused for a moment before stripping down to his Calvins. Ciara didn't know which shocked her more: Heidi's totally uncharacteristic behavior or AJ's amazing physique. Either way, she was speechless. She flashed back to getting dressed for the party and winced as she thought of the plain white bra and underwear she'd put on. She might as well just hop in the pool naked. The old Ciara might have been into that, but it looked like the new Ciara would have to keep her clothes on. As AJ ran to join Heidi in the pool, she figured she'd be spending the night high and dry—literally *and* figuratively.

"Looks like *someone's* having fun," a voice said close to Ciara's left ear. She turned to see Kevin standing next to her, staring down at AJ and Heidi splashing around in the water.

"Yeah, really." Ciara sighed. She looked at the tiny pile Heidi's shirt, shoes, and miniskirt had made on one of the deck chairs. "I guess Heidi's changed a lot since the one-piece swimsuit days, huh?"

"It's only recently." Kevin shook his head in confusion. "She was just this totally normal, semi-conservative girl until the last month of school, and suddenly—*bam!*—she's like something out of *Girls Gone Wild*."

"Why the change?" Ciara asked.

"I don't really know . . . but I have a theory," Kevin said, wiggling his eyebrows.

"Care to dish?"

"Well, she was dating this guy Jude for like two weeks back in March," Kevin said. "She was crazy about him, but then he dumped her for this other girl, Princess. Princess was a bit more of a party animal."

"Sounds more like purebred royalty to me," Ciara quipped. "So Heidi decided that's what guys go for?" She couldn't help thinking that Heidi wasn't too far off track—the guys back in LA had loved her wild, dare-to-do-anything streak.

"Yeah." Kevin stopped smiling and his voice grew heavy. "I don't think it's the most brilliant decision she ever made."

"So you liked the old Heidi better," Ciara said sympathetically.

"I thought the old Heidi liked me," Kevin said. "But it looks like the new Heidi is all about AJ."

They both watched as Heidi shot up from under the water and struggled to dunk AJ, her chest smooshed against the top of his head. Just seeing the way AJ grabbed her waist in retaliation made Ciara's insides writhe with envy.

"It must be rough having someone switch lanes on you like that," Ciara said.

"It wasn't exactly highlight reel material," Kevin joked. He motioned for Ciara to join him at one of the white wrought-iron tables surrounding the pool. A votive candle floating in a small bowl of water flicked light onto their faces.

"So what happened?" Ciara asked. Kevin lowered his eyes, looking embarrassed. "I'm sorry," Ciara added quickly. "You don't have to tell me if you don't want. I mean, we haven't even seen each other in years."

"Nah, that's cool," Kevin said, his eyes briefly meeting hers. "Me and Heidi were spending a lot of time together. Nothing major—I mean, she was like this good girl, so it's not like anything was even *happening*. Mostly I was just helping her get over Jude. But then AJ and Marlene break up and it's like Heidi's style goes all Paris Hilton in two weeks flat, she starts going on about how she's trying to 'get in touch with her wild side,' and she drops me like a hot potato."

"That's gotta sting," Ciara said. She could sympathize—seeing Heidi all over *her* perfect guy made her skin prickle.

"Like I said, I'd prefer if they left it out of the B-Dizzy Crew documentary," Kevin joked darkly.

"So what happened with AJ and Marlene?" Ciara asked, hoping it didn't sound too much like she was digging for information.

"Well, as you've probably gathered, they dated for

more than two years, then broke up," Kevin said. Ciara nodded for him to continue. "So, like, we started the B-Dizzy Crew about a year ago. I've been spinning records a lot longer than that, and one day AJ was over at my place while I was scratching and he started freestyling over it and was immediately like, 'Dude, we have something here—we have to do this.' As soon as we started getting gigs, AJ's ego inflated and Marlene just couldn't deal. She's such a strong personality, it's like there wasn't room in the world for both of them."

"Do you think he's over her?" Ciara asked carefully.

"Well, he's not exactly the type to sit around crying into a pint of Ben and Jerry's," Kevin said. "Especially with the attention he's getting these days. I think he's mostly just focusing on his music—but if the right girl came along, I bet AJ wouldn't turn her down."

"Good," Ciara blurted. As soon as she realized what she'd said, her hands flew to her mouth. She had just given *way* too much away.

"Uh-oh," Kevin said, smiling wryly. "Looks like you're hot for AJ too."

Ciara's face was so red she was sure Kevin could tell even in the dim candlelight. "I've always had a soft spot for emcees," she admitted.

"Isn't that the way it always is?" Kevin stared up at the stars, shaking his head in mock exasperation. "The emcees get all the love, and the DJs get squat."

"You could say the same about the girls who strip down to their skivvies and jump in the pool versus the girls who stay dressed on the deck," Ciara pointed out.

"Touché."

They both watched as Heidi climbed out of the pool, her butt twitching in her soaked underpants. She shot AJ an inviting glance before taking off for the pool house. AJ turned and swam underwater to the deep end, his shoulders gleaming in the light of a nearby tiki torch as he climbed the submerged metal ladder and wandered off toward the pool house as well.

Kevin and Ciara let out simultaneous sighs.

"Isn't it ironic," Kevin observed. "They seem to want each other—and we both want them."

"Maybe if we work together, we can make things work in our favor," Ciara mused.

"Yeah, good one," Kevin said. "It would probably be easier to change the laws of physics."

"No, seriously!" Ciara could feel herself getting excited, the way she always did when she came up with a good idea for the student council or a valid argument for the debate club. "I mean, they haven't even gotten together yet. Right now, they're just flirting."

"We *hope*," Kevin interjected, shooting a glance toward the door of the pool house.

"Well, yeah. But it's still in the very early stages. I mean, you're AJ's best friend, right? And I'll be working with Heidi all summer. That means we have the opportunity to bend their ears a lot."

"You mean, you'd talk me up to Heidi all day at work?" Kevin asked, starting to catch on.

"Right. And you'd do the same with AJ."

A tiny smile began to stretch the corners of Kevin's mouth.

"Not only that," Ciara continued, "but I can find out exactly what Heidi really wants in a guy. If she's wild about daisies, you show up with a bouquet of them the next day. If she digs men with mustaches, you grow a mustache."

"Hey, easy." Kevin laughed. "I'm not growing a mustache for *anyone*. I don't even think I can—Korean guys aren't exactly renowned for their lush facial hair."

"Okay, you can skip the mustache," Ciara conceded through her giggles. "But you know what I mean."

"Do you really think this will work?" Kevin asked. He still sounded skeptical.

"I've found that if I put my mind to something, I can generally make it happen," Ciara said firmly. "But it will only work if you're in it one hundred percent. Are you?"

"I guess so," Kevin said. "I've had a thing for Heidi since ninth grade."

He reached out his hand and Ciara shook it.

"Woo-ha!" Kevin whooped.

"Huh?" Ciara asked. Had Kevin really just *whooped*?

Kevin looked embarrassed. "Woo-ha. It's what I say when I'm psyched about something. It's from this old Get Set V.O.P. track I dug up—they're like this totally obscure hip-hop/jazz fusion group, but I love the song. I'll play it for you sometime."

"Woo-ha," Ciara repeated, smiling. "I like that. That's what we're calling this plan, okay?"

"Woo-ha?" Kevin asked. "So I'll be like, 'Yo, Ciara, how's Woo-ha going?'"

"It needs to sound more official than that so we take it seriously," Ciara said. "How about *Operation* Woo-ha?"

"Operation Woo-ha," Kevin repeated. "I like the sound of that."

"Well, then, here goes nothing," Ciara said, raising her fist in the air. Kevin brought his hand up to meet hers in a power salute.

"Woo-ha," they said at the same time. There was a moment of somber contemplation as they each pondered the future of their scheme. Then they both dissolved into laughter.

Chapter Five

Woo-ha-ha, woo-woo-ha-ha, woo-ha!
— *Get Set V.O.P.*

"What are you two talking about?" AJ asked, approaching Kevin and Ciara. They'd been deep in conversation about Operation Woo-ha, but the sight of AJ bare-chested, with a big beach towel draped loosely around his hips, temporarily sent all of Ciara's plans orbiting toward outer space.

"Oh, we were just discussing the difference between the East Coast and West Coast sound in the mid-nineties," Kevin said smoothly. "Hey, Ciara knows a *lot* about hip-hop. She really impressed me—and you know what a snob I am."

"Get this guy in a record shop and forget about dragging him out again," AJ joked.

"Where's Heidi?" Kevin asked, looking around.

"In the sauna," AJ said absently. "It got too hot for me in there."

Ciara and Kevin exchanged significant looks. Just how "hot" had it really gotten? they wondered.

"Wow, yeah, I forgot D-John had one of those," Kevin said, getting up quickly. "I'm gonna go check it out."

Ciara's heart thumped against her rib cage as she realized she was momentarily alone with AJ. She was usually so good at talking to guys, but AJ's huge brown eyes left her speechless.

"So you really liked the show?" AJ asked while she was still trying to find her tongue.

"Oh yeah!" she said quickly. "That song about your first car was hilarious. I love that you can inject humor into your rhymes but still make them meaningful. Honestly, I think you guys could totally blow up."

AJ's shoulders straightened with pride. "That's my dream," he said. "It's nice to have someone believe in me. Sometimes I think everyone's just humoring me, like, 'Yeah, sure, you'll be huge. But don't start picking out mansions yet.'"

"I think people should follow their dreams," Ciara said firmly. "I mean, I want to be an entertainment lawyer, so I study my butt off. Maybe I'll be representing you someday."

"That would be sweet." AJ leaned closer to her, his eyes sparkling in the candlelight. The new Chris Brown song wafted through the speakers, and everything around them seemed to intensify: the smell of gardenias; the flickering candlelight; and the soft, warm caress of the summer night air. "You know, it really is great to see you again."

"It's good to see you too," Ciara breathed. Their faces were inches apart. Who needed Operation Woo-ha when they clearly had this much chemistry?

"Having you dancing up onstage with us was amazing," AJ continued, his eyes sparkling like live embers. "And talking to you is even better. It's like you really know where I'm coming from."

"It's easy when you're so good at what you do," Ciara said. AJ's nose was practically touching hers, and she wanted to kiss him more than anything else in the world. But instead, she pulled back. AJ looked confused for a moment but then leaned away as well, letting the moment pass. He looked maybe even a little relieved. Could it be that the thought of kissing her had made him nervous too?

Just then, Heidi came bounding up to them. Like AJ, she was wrapped in a towel, her damp platinum hair clinging to the sides of her face.

"AJ!" she squealed. "There you are. I thought I lost you to the party gods!"

"Nah." AJ scooted his chair back, away from Ciara. "I'm still around."

Mixed feelings of relief and disappointment washed through Ciara. It was so unlike her not to jump on a perfect moment like that to kiss a hottie. On the one hand, she was proud of herself for being strong enough to hold out on kissing until she'd established something real with AJ. She was also happy that Heidi hadn't caught her hitting on the guy she was obviously after. She made a mental note to talk to Heidi at work the next day and start gently easing her attention toward Kevin instead.

Then again, she kind of wished she'd gotten at least one kiss. Just one. Just to see what it felt like to kiss the hottest emcee on the West Coast. Why hadn't she let him kiss her? Had the new Ciara really taken hold of her that fast? Maybe it was a preservation instinct—the slower she took things with AJ, the longer she hoped their relationship would last.

Chill out, she told herself, stretching back in her chair and smiling at both of them. *The summer's just getting started. You've got plenty of time.*

Chapter Six

Let's walk to the bridge, now meet me halfway
—OutKast

Hey, John, I'm going to take five," Ciara called to the manager, hanging her visor on its peg in the tiny locker room assigned to the beach club café staff. She grabbed her bag and ran down to the beach, eager to dip her toes in the surf.

She was still flying from the night before: everything from the show to her almost kiss with AJ convinced her that Santa Barbara was the right place to be. When her cell rang, she grabbed for it, hoping it would be AJ calling to ask her out or even Kevin reporting on the progress of Operation Woo-Ha.

When she saw the name on the screen, her excitement deflated like a popped balloon. Her mom was the last person she wanted to hear from.

"Hi, honey," Maria Simmons said in her best crisp, professional voice. "I was just calling to make sure you got settled okay."

"Yeah, everything's fine." Ciara couldn't help adding that her dad had taken time off work to meet her and cook her lunch.

"That's nice." Her mom's voice sounded drawn in on itself, as if she were cold and clasping a jacket around her shoulders. "So what are you doing with yourself up there?"

"I got a job," Ciara told her. "Working at the beach club."

"Good for you," her mom said. "I'm proud of you. It's your first real job!"

"My first job where I make money," Ciara corrected her. "The internship and being a CIT were both a lot of work."

"Right," her mom conceded. There was a long pause.

"So how are things in LA?" Ciara asked to be polite. Not because she actually wanted to know.

"Things are fine," her mom said. She took a deep breath. "I put the house on the market."

A wave of sadness coursed through Ciara. They'd

lived in that house since she was five. She loved her room with the sloping ceiling and her desk overlooking the shady backyard.

"I'm looking at apartments," her mom continued. "Of course, I'll find one with a nice room for you."

"Cool," Ciara said dully. Part of her wanted to tell her not to bother—if things went as planned, she wouldn't be coming back in the fall anyway. But the words caught in her throat.

"I need to get going," she said instead. "I'm on a five-minute work break."

They said good-bye and she trudged back up the sand to the café, realizing as she stepped into the office that she hadn't dipped her toes in the ocean after all.

"What's wrong?" Heidi asked, slipping in to grab a fresh pen from the drawer of the tiny metal desk.

"Oh, nothing," Ciara said, realizing she must have been frowning. "Just family drama. No big deal."

"I'm sorry—I hope everything works out," Heidi said. She sat down next to Ciara on the bench. "You got plans for our day off tomorrow?"

"Day off?" Ciara asked. She'd barely had time to look at the schedule since she started working.

"Sunday, remember?" Heidi nudged her in the ribs, smiling. "The café's closed."

"Oh yeah," Ciara said, feeling silly for not remembering.

"I guess I'll take a book down to the beach. I've barely had time to catch any rays."

Heidi swung her legs back and forth like a little kid. She seemed almost nervous. "That sounds like fun," she said. "But if you want to come to Six Flags instead, I'm going with AJ and Kevin and maybe Marlene, if she wants to come."

"Wow, thanks," Ciara said, smiling. "I'll totally hit Six Flags with you guys."

"Cool." Heidi got up to check on one of her tables. "We're going in Kevin's car—I'll ask if he can pick you up."

"Oh, that'll be great," Ciara said. "Kevin's so sweet and considerate, isn't he?"

"Sure," Heidi said, giving Ciara a funny look as she breezed out onto the deck, where diners were starting to call her name. Ciara wondered if she'd been too obvious, or maybe should have said something else. Would sweet, considerate Kevin really be that appealing to Heidi the self-proclaimed wild girl?

Ciara smiled. Her head was already fast-forwarding to the next day. What a perfect opportunity to put Operation Woo-ha into effect! She craned her head to make sure Heidi had really gone, then grabbed her phone to send Kevin a quick text message.

*   *   *

"Ready to Woo-ha?" Kevin asked, bounding up the steps to the café.

"You bet!" Ciara grinned. She'd changed from her uniform into shorts and a tank top and couldn't wait to spend the remaining daylight hours on the beach. "Was this whole Six Flags thing your idea?"

"Kinda sorta," Kevin admitted. "I mentioned to AJ that it's been a while since we've gone there and he was like, 'Let's go tomorrow.' That guy's a maniac for scary rides. Another thing you should know about him."

"Fine, as long as they don't flip upside down," Ciara noted. "My stomach just can't handle it."

"We'll see what we can do about keeping him off the Viper," Kevin said as they walked together down the beach.

"You really think this will work?" Ciara asked, luxuriating in the feel of the cool sand between her toes.

"Yeah, it'll be great. You'll be strapped in next to him on all these rides—plenty of opportunities for groping." Kevin wiggled his eyebrows.

"I'll leave the groping to you and Heidi." Ciara laughed. "Although I might grab his arm or something if I get really, really scared . . ."

"That's the idea," Kevin said.

Ciara ran down to the water's edge and let the warm Pacific surf lap at her ankles. "Heidi and I had a little talk about boys during the lull after the lunch shift today," she said.

"Yeah?" Kevin stooped to remove his Adidases and roll up his jeans before joining her in the surf. "And what did she say?"

"The good news is, she's not exclusively focused on AJ. The bad news is, she's all over the map. She mentioned like twelve guys she thinks are cute."

"Let me guess—I wasn't one of them," Kevin said morosely.

"Not specifically," Ciara said, trying to be diplomatic. "But you're really funny, and she did say she loves guys who make her laugh."

"You should be a spin doctor," Kevin said, grinning.

A large wave came rolling toward them and they both scampered back. "So you didn't happen to drop my name into any conversations with AJ today, did you?" Ciara asked.

Kevin frowned. "I tried. But all he wanted to talk about was the band. He thinks we should have a marketing strategy—I think we should just chill and make good music."

"A marketing strategy can be important if you want to make it big," Ciara said. "And until you get the attention of an A and R guy at a major label, you have to promote, promote, promote."

Kevin grimaced. "I hate promoting. If the music is good, won't people just want to listen to it?"

"Do you have any idea how much good music is out there?" Ciara asked. "You need to get out and push yourself if you want to make it big. Didn't you see *Hustle and Flow*?"

"Twice," Kevin admitted. "In the theater. AJ still beat me, though—he went three times. He has parts of it memorized."

"He's so driven." Ciara sighed. "I love that."

"Hey, we're driven too!" Kevin protested. "We're putting the first stage of Operation Woo-ha into action tomorrow. If that's not drive, I don't know what is."

"You're right," Ciara said happily. She was excited about the chance to spend the whole next day with AJ and suddenly felt so full of energy she did a cartwheel on the empty beach. A curious seagull swooped down to see what all the fuss was about, then left after realizing it didn't involve food.

Kevin chuckled at her sudden athletic display. "Bring that kind of energy to Six Flags tomorrow," he said, "and we'll be all set."

Chapter Seven

Big teddy bears, cotton candy everywhere
We can do this thing every day, every year
Come on and talk to me
Now walk with me
Think about it—this how it ought to be

—Lil' Romeo

Ciara had never been such a wreck over what to wear to an amusement park. In fact, getting worked up over an outfit had never been her style: she liked soft, vintage-looking clothes that she could move and dance in and figured that as long as she was comfortable, boys would find her hot. She had always laughed at girls who went wobbling around in stilettos and miniskirts, looking like they were going to fall over any second—why would any guy find that attractive?

But on the beach the day before, Kevin had told her that AJ went for girls who didn't mind showing a little skin from time to time. Her usual high-necked, cap-sleeved T-shirts from Anthropologie and vintage uniform pieces clearly weren't going to cut it. Sighing, Ciara peeled off the seventies-style Boy Scout shirt she'd just tried on and flung it onto the bed. Digging through her dresser, she unearthed a bright purple halter top that Em had brought back from her family vacation. *Hawaii* was scrawled across the front in electric blue script, and it was cut to show way more belly than Ciara was used to. Slipping it on, she looked in the mirror and gasped. Paired with the denim miniskirt that had looked perfectly demure with the Boy Scout shirt, the halter top made her look like an extra in a 50 Cent video. All she needed to complete the outfit was a pair of Ecko Red crocodile stilettos and some bling.

Ciara laughed to herself as she replaced the skirt with her favorite pair of worn Diesel jeans and a woven leather belt. Much better. The shirt still showed off way more skin than she was used to, but at least her tummy was smooth and flat from hours of swim team practice.

A car horn honked outside and Ciara ran downstairs, hopping into the backseat of Kevin's Acura next to Heidi.

"Where's Marlene?" she asked everyone in the car. But the music booming through the speakers was so loud that apparently only Heidi heard her.

"She couldn't make it," Heidi said quietly, leaning in so close that her breath ruffled Ciara's hair. "Something about having to work."

"That's too bad," Ciara said. "It seems like she never gets to come out and have any fun."

"Yeah, it's a bummer." Heidi shrugged, looking out the window.

"Totally," Ciara agreed. It was too bad that Marlene wasn't going to be there, but at the same time, it would make Operation Woo-ha that much easier. Was she a jerk for having those kinds of thoughts? She told herself not to worry about it—it was her day off, and she should just relax and have fun.

"I love this song!" she shouted over Jurassic 5's "Freedom," which shook the car slightly from the extra-large speakers Kevin had installed in the trunk.

AJ, who was riding shotgun, peered around the side of the passenger's seat to grin at her. "Aren't they amazing?" he asked, his chocolate-brown eyes sending beads of sweat popping out on her forehead.

You're amazing, Ciara found herself thinking. His eyes alone put all the boys back at Westwood Prep to shame.

"Perfect summer music," she agreed instead.

"And today's a perfect summer day," Heidi chirped next to her in the backseat. "Who's ready to ride some roller coasters?"

"Me!" everyone shouted at the same time. Kevin stepped on the gas as they sped onto the highway, the ocean receding beneath them, the sky a perfect cerulean blue. As AJ and Kevin gabbed away about their crew up front, Ciara glanced over at Heidi and realized she wasn't the only one who had dared to show some skin. Heidi had on a tiny white terry jumper with rainbow stripes down the sides—it had a cute retro feel and looked like something a little kid might wear, but hugged her curves perfectly. The top two buttons were undone to reveal enough cleavage to make any guy stop and stare, and for the first time ever, Ciara wished she had more to work with than a 32B. She usually felt comfortable with her body, but something about AJ made her suddenly care a whole lot more than usual about how she looked.

Heidi looked over at Ciara and grinned. "I'm so glad you decided to come," she said. "It's nice to get to hang out with you outside of work."

"Yeah," Ciara agreed. Inside, she felt bad. Heidi thought she had come along because of her invitation. She had no idea it was all about getting closer to the hottie in the front seat.

By the time they pulled into the massive parking lot at Six Flags, Heidi had reapplied her Sephora plumping lip gloss six times, and her lips looked as large and shiny as the inside of a watermelon. "I am *so* ready to hit some rides," she said as she hopped down to the pavement, the skirt of her jumper catching the wind and billowing around her legs for a moment like a parachute.

"I'm just happy to be out of the car." Ciara stretched her hands over her head so the halter top rode farther up on her tummy. She caught AJ staring at her for a moment longer than necessary and allowed herself an inner cheer.

"Let's go on Scream! first!" AJ said as they entered the park, skirting around a group of toddlers with the remains of ice-cream sandwiches caked to the sides of their mouths.

Ciara's stomach jolted. The last time she had visited the park, she remembered staring up at the tiny passengers waving their legs in the air like beetles flung onto their backs, their screams drifting down from several dozen stories above. At the time, she'd politely told Em there was no freakin' way she was going on that thing, and Em had understood. But this time was different. She was with AJ, and she certainly wasn't going to stay on the ground like a nervous puppy while he went on the ride.

"Looks like fun!" she said, trying to sound enthusiastic. "Let's do it!"

"Think you can handle it, bro?" AJ asked Kevin. Ciara thought momentarily that he was being kind of condescending, but just then AJ's arm brushed hers and she forgot all about it. Had anyone ever had a heart attack over being touched by a boy before? If she didn't go into coronary arrest over the skin-on-skin contact, she just might on the roller coaster. Either way, it was doubtful she'd make it out of the park alive.

But looking up into AJ's smiling eyes made her feel like everything would be all right as long as he was next to her. She smiled and leaned even closer to him, breathing in his sexy, musky smell. No matter how scared she was of going on Scream!, she wouldn't trade where she was standing at that moment for anywhere else in the world.

"Nervous?" Kevin asked Heidi behind them. Out of the corner of her eye, she could see him struggling to get up the courage to touch her. Unfortunately, he wasn't quite as smooth as AJ and his hands stayed in the pockets of his jeans.

"Nah!" Heidi said, practically bouncing up and down with excitement. "I love roller coasters—the scarier, the better. Bring it on!"

"You sound just like Marlene," AJ said. "It's too bad she couldn't make it today—she loves this place."

Ciara fervently wished she felt the same way about roller coasters as Heidi, Marlene, and seemingly every person in the universe other than her. As they inched closer in line, she could feel her palms grow damp with sweat. To distract herself, she asked AJ about his marketing plan for the B-Dizzy Crew.

AJ's eyes shone with excitement. "I know we have the right sound to make it big," he said. "But I want to make sure we stand out visually, you know? So I talked to this friend of mine who's going to CalArts next year to study graphic design and I'm having him make a logo for us. I want it to look kind of dizzy, like you get a little dizzy when you see it, you know?"

"That's a great idea," Ciara said. "It's cool that you're doing something other than that bang-bang, bling-bling gangsta stuff."

"Yeah, well, we gotta have a little of that too, you know?" AJ laughed. "I mean, that's what sells these days. But it's hard when you're a good middle-class kid from Santa Barbara. It's not exactly Compton."

"Maybe you should start a gang to boost your street cred," Ciara joked.

"Yeah, right." AJ snorted. "Me and DJ Kev-lar can shake down middle schoolers for milk money. Hard-*core*."

Ciara was so busy giggling that she didn't realize they had reached the front of the line. Suddenly, she found herself face-to-face with a row of seats with no floor or sides.

"Come on," said AJ, nudging her toward the ride. Her heart sped up as she climbed in, her butt shifting uncomfortably on the blue molded plastic. It felt too big and slippery, as if she could fly right off and go careening four hundred feet from the top of the ride to her certain death on the mountain below.

"Arms in," the operator grunted roughly as he snapped the safety bars down over her lap and shoulders, pinning her hips to the seat. She glanced at the track ahead, which ascended almost straight up before dropping off in a terrifying series of loops and corkscrews. Why had she agreed to do this? She had always hated rides that went upside down. In addition to scaring the crap out of her, they made her feel dizzy and nauseous for hours.

"This is going to be fun," AJ said, reaching out and squeezing the top of her hand, which she realized had gone nearly white from gripping the safety bars so hard.

"I guess . . . ," she said shakily as the ride began rumbling beneath them. She wanted to yell for the operator to come back and let her off, but it was too late. They were slowly climbing the track, the park spreading out below them until the lines of people at each attraction were as tiny and colorful as sprinkles on top of an ice-cream cone. She wished the ride would just stay like that, chugging gradually upward. She liked being high in the air. She didn't even mind going fast. It was the upside-down part she was dreading.

They hovered at the summit for a moment, and she took in the green of the treetops below them and AJ's gorgeous almond-shaped eyes sparkling in the sunlight before the world dropped off beneath her and they went plummeting down the track, her breath and stomach still somewhere up at the top. She shut her eyes tight as wind rushed against her face, and then she felt her insides twist as they went shooting up into a loop. She heard herself whimpering.

The ride seemed to last for hours. Every time she thought it was close to being over, another loop loomed ahead and her stomach flopped like a dying fish, threatening to shoot its contents out her throat and all over AJ's lap. By the time it was over, she barely had the energy to lift the safety bars off her lap and shoulders. Her arms and legs felt sticky and weak, and she could hardly look at AJ as he held out his hand to help her climb out of the seat.

"You all right?" he asked. "You look kind of green."

Ciara did her best to put on a brave, cheerful face, but it must have come across as more of a grimace. She grasped AJ's arm as they headed toward the blacktop beyond the ride's exit gate, but it was more for support than out of lust. Hot as AJ was, the only thing she could keep her mind on was not puking all over his Pumas.

"Omigod, wasn't that amazing!" Heidi gasped, bouncing up and down as they approached. "Those loops were killer. I thought I was going to slide between the bars and go flying through the air!"

Just the thought made Ciara's knees tremble.

"Are you okay?" Kevin asked, seeing her face. "You look like maybe you didn't have so much fun."

"Oh no," Ciara assured him, trying for a smile. "That was a good time."

"Cool," said Heidi, already leading the group toward another line that snaked through a maze of metal barriers. "Who's up for Tatsu?"

"Me!" AJ said enthusiastically. "I hope it's scarier than the last one."

"It's supposed to be the most terrifying ride in the history of roller coasters," Kevin assured him. "It starts with, like, a two-hundred-foot drop or something, and your arms and feet aren't strapped in, so you feel like you're flying. And then you do the whole thing backwards!"

"Sweet!" Heidi yelped.

Ciara glanced up at Tatsu. The red-and-orange track twisted sadistically above them in a series of corkscrew turns that seemed to defy physics. As she stared up, the train went zooming by faster than a Porsche on the LA freeway, a mess of wiggling legs and arms and zombie movie screams.

"Oh no," Ciara groaned softly before she could stop herself.

"What's wrong?" AJ asked, his eyes wide with concern.

"Nothing," Ciara said quickly. "I'm fine."

"Are you scared or something?" Heidi asked. It was obvious from her tone that she was just trying to be nice, but Ciara took it as a challenge anyway.

"No!" she found herself saying. "It looks like a blast." As she spoke, she wondered what she was getting herself into. Her entire body still felt wobbly from the last ride, and her stomach definitely was not in the best shape. Was she really going to force herself to do it again?

As they got closer to the front of the line, Ciara could feel her courage flagging. She just didn't want to put herself through that again, no matter how hot AJ was. It was that simple. As the group in front of them climbed into the seats and kicked playfully at the empty air in front of them, Ciara's heart began to race. She wiped her soaking palms on her jeans, realizing she was close to tears.

"You know what?" she said suddenly as the roller coaster began to rumble, bringing the car in front of them high above their heads. "I think I'm going to sit this one out." She spat the words out as quickly as possible before she could change her mind.

"If you can't handle the heat, better stay away from the fire," AJ joked. Ciara felt a twinge of annoyance fight its way through her anxiety. Backing down was hard enough as it was—she didn't need AJ cracking lame jokes at her expense.

"There's only so much masochism a girl can take," she shot back acidly.

"Yeah, sorry," AJ said. "Listen, do you mind if I still go? We've been waiting on line for a while."

"No, go for it," Ciara assured him, her heart sinking. She'd secretly been hoping he would offer to keep her company on the ground. Sure, it was an unrealistic expectation, given how much AJ liked roller coasters—still, it seemed to her like they'd really been clicking.

"I'll go on with you!" Heidi volunteered before the words were even out of Ciara's mouth.

"Cool." AJ grinned at Heidi—the grin Ciara had come to think of as "hers"—and she felt her spirit sink as low as the gum stuck to the walkway.

"See you when you hit the ground," she said, trying to sound cheerful. She turned and ducked under the metal barrier, making her way toward a picnic table at the base of a nearby tree.

"Wait up!" She turned to see Kevin vaulting over the barrier behind her.

"What are you doing?" she asked.

"Keeping you company," he said, catching up with her.

"You don't have to do that," she said as they walked together to the picnic table. She didn't realize until they sat down how good it was to get off her still-shaky legs.

"It's fine," Kevin assured her. "I think I'd rather sit down here and talk to you than be up there screaming my head off, anyway."

"Thanks." Ciara couldn't believe how sweet Kevin was being—she knew that he'd rather be on the roller coaster with Heidi than talking to her. "If I'd gone on that ride, I totally would have puked on his lap, and then I would have *really* blown my chances."

Kevin shrugged. "There are better ways to show a guy you care than vomiting on him," he conceded. "It seemed like he was into you while we were all on line, though."

"Really?" Ciara felt her mood brighten.

"Um, hello—he was standing so close to you, I'm surprised he didn't step on your foot. And the way he was looking at you in that shirt was not exactly brotherly love."

"Oh, stop," she said playfully. But she could feel her cheeks getting hot.

"No, seriously," Kevin assured her. "You look hot."

"Well—thanks." Ciara glanced at him out of the corner of her eye. She wanted to see if he was joking or not, but all she could see was her reflection in his mirrored sunglasses. His *ugly* mirrored sunglasses.

"You know," she said, "I think you should lose those shades."

"Yeah?" Kevin reached up to fiddle self-consciously with the frames but didn't take them off.

Ciara nodded. The more she looked at Kevin's face, the truer that seemed. The glasses were too circular for his square jaw, and the mirrors distorted her face when she tried to look in his eyes, making her focus on her own reflection instead of on him.

"I bet Heidi would be more into you if she could see your eyes," Ciara said. "The mirrors make you seem kind of detached—plus you look like a cop."

"Ew." Kevin's nose wrinkled in disgust.

"There's a sunglasses stand right over there," Ciara suggested, pointing. "Come with me."

Although it was painted to look like an old-fashioned buggy, the racks on the Shade Shack gleamed with steel, plastic, and UV-resistant coatings.

"You want something that will flatter your face, not hide it," Ciara said. She held up a pair of square black frames. "Try these."

Kevin shrugged and swapped his *CSI* shades for the new ones. Ciara tried to stifle a giggle as he peered into one of the mirrors affixed to the side of the cart, but a snort leaked out around her hand.

"Unless Heidi's an underground Elvis Costello fan, I don't think she's really going to go for these," Kevin said. He tried on several more pairs that he and Ciara dubbed, respectively, Green Day Visits the Library, R. Kelly with a Hangover, and Grandma Gone Bad.

"How about these?" Kevin asked. Ciara looked up to see him sporting a simple pair of steel rims with a light gray tint. They made him look older and more sophisticated, but also hip: like the kind of guy who would take you to a Japanese-Brazilian fusion restaurant and then to an underground club where your favorite band was performing a secret show.

"Perfect," she said.

"All right—we have a winner," Kevin said, paying for the glasses.

"Don't forget these," the guy at the stand yelled after them, holding out the old, mirrored pair.

"Toss 'em," Kevin called back. Ciara could tell the new shades had given his self-esteem a little boost—his chin seemed higher and his shoulders more square and alert. She allowed herself a small, triumphant smile.

"Do you think Heidi will notice?" Kevin asked.

"I don't see how she couldn't," Ciara assured him. "But can I give you some advice? Next time you want to put your arm around her, do it! I could tell you wanted to when we were all waiting on line . . . so why didn't you?"

"I dunno—I get shy around her," Kevin said. "I mean, it's not like that with other girls. With anyone else, I would have just gone for it, but not Heidi. She's special."

"Special how?"

"She's just . . . so much sweeter and more innocent than other girls. I mean, I know she claims to be going through this wild-woman phase right now, but when you really know her, you can tell it's all an act. She's still got this vulnerability shining through that drives me nuts. Makes me want to protect her."

"That's so sweet," Ciara said wistfully. She couldn't imagine a boy ever saying something like that about her. She prided herself on being able to take care of herself, but the ability to make boys want to protect her sounded oddly appealing.

A stream of people came barreling through Tatsu's exit, and Ciara watched as a roly-poly boy with carrot-colored hair and a face like strained beets staggered into the bushes and upchucked what looked like a few pounds of cotton candy. "I am never going on that ride again," he said miserably as he rejoined his family, wiping his mouth on the back of his hand.

Ciara and Kevin turned to each other and laughed. "I'm not sorry we missed it," Ciara admitted.

Heidi came bounding out of the exit, AJ close at her heels.

"Omigod, that was so fun!" Heidi cried, dashing up to them and jumping up and down. "Wasn't that awesome, AJ?"

"It was pretty sweet," AJ agreed, loping up behind her. He draped his arm casually over Heidi's shoulders, and Ciara felt a bubble of jealousy rise in her throat.

"Hey, cute glasses," Heidi said, peering up at Kevin and grinning. "You get those while we were on the ride?"

"Yeah," Kevin said through a pleased smile. "Ciara talked me into it. She said the old ones made me look like a cop."

"Good going, Ciara." AJ laughed, removing his arm from around Heidi's shoulders to give Ciara a high five. Her heart soared as his hand met hers in midair, and she savored the sting of his flesh on her palm.

"Totally," Heidi agreed. "You look way cute in those." She giggled, and Kevin turned about thirty different shades of red. Fortunately, Heidi didn't notice. She had already returned her attention to AJ.

"Want to do some more coasters?" she asked, taking his hand and swinging it back and forth like a child pestering her parents for ice cream. "Can we? Please?"

AJ smiled down at her. "I'm game," he said. The shiver Ciara felt when he slapped her hand froze inside her. Was he really going to ditch her again?

"What's your favorite?" Heidi asked.

"I love the Psychlone," Ciara volunteered. Mostly because it never went upside down once, but there was no need to spill that little detail.

Heidi wrinkled her nose. "Too tame," she said dismissively. "I want something that will give me whiplash. How about the Viper?"

"I think that's still my favorite." AJ grinned. "I'm down if you are."

"Let's do it!" Heidi said.

"What about you guys?" AJ asked, turning to Kevin and Ciara. "Viper?"

"I don't think so," Ciara said, trying not to sound too defeated.

Kevin shook his head as well. "I think there's a bluegrass group playing on one of the stages," he said. "Maybe we'll go check that out instead."

"Bluegrass?" Ciara asked incredulously.

Kevin grinned sheepishly. "Music is music," he said. "I'm equal opportunity as long as it's good."

"You're crazy," AJ said affectionately. "Just don't go mixing any of that into my beats."

The four of them headed toward the Viper, Heidi

skipping along happily as Ciara concentrated on not dragging her feet on the ground in frustration. She and Kevin exchanged defeated looks as they dropped AJ and Heidi in line for the Viper. Neither of them needed to spell out the obvious—that Heidi was clearly all about AJ.

Kevin led the way to a small wooden stage, on which several bearded men in flannel shirts picked at acoustic guitars and banjos. A small crowd of mostly older music fans (probably the parents and grandparents of kids who were off on the rides) nodded to the music, sedate smiles on their faces.

"I'm surprised you're into this kind of stuff," Ciara said, mostly to distract them from their disappointment.

Kevin tapped his foot along to the beat. "Bluegrass has a bad rep," he said. "You think of it as backwoods country-bumpkin music, but it actually takes a lot of skill and precision to play. Listen to how they all work together."

As Ciara watched, the fiddle player launched into a complicated solo. Behind him, the rest of the group kept up a thumping beat. "I guess you do have to be pretty talented," she admitted.

"It bothers me that people can be so closed-minded about music," Kevin said. "Like AJ will only listen to hip-hop. But to really understand hip-hop, you have to know about jazz and funk and soul and R and B. Even bluegrass. You close yourself off to a lot of amazing sounds if you only listen to one genre."

Ciara had to admit that the group's enthusiasm was contagious. She found herself smiling when the fiddle solo ended and the rest of the group launched into a raucous chorus.

"This is definitely more fun than losing my lunch on a loop-de-loop," she said. It was also something that Em would be into. Whenever she landed on a weird radio station, she'd always give it at least a three-song shot.

"I'd rather catch some good tunes than have to hang on to some safety bar for dear life any day," Kevin agreed.

A cascade of familiar giggles made them both whirl around. AJ and Heidi were approaching, doubled over in laughter and clutching each other for support.

"Could we look any worse?" Heidi asked, holding up a glossy photograph in the cheap cardboard commemorative frame from the Viper's photo booth. Ciara leaned in for a look. Heidi's platinum hair was tangled in the wind and AJ's long, dark eyelashes seemed plastered against his face. They both had their mouths open in a combination of fear and laughter, and she could see the gold cap on one of AJ's molars.

Ciara's stomach flipped with disappointment. They were holding hands on top of the safety bar. She stared at the photograph for what seemed like a very long time, unable to look up at AJ, afraid he'd see the loss and rejection etched clearly across her face.

"I can't believe you paid for that picture," Kevin was saying, his voice carefully neutral to hide his own emotions.

"This day's been really fun," AJ said.

"Yeah, I wanted something to remember it by," Heidi agreed. Her face was flushed, and Ciara wondered if it was just leftover adrenaline from the ride or if something more than hand-holding had happened on the Viper.

A trace of the nausea she'd felt on Scream! earlier came whirling back, and she reminded herself that the picture didn't prove anything.

"Hey, I'm starving. Anyone up for a corn dog?" Heidi asked.

Kevin agreed enthusiastically, and Ciara nodded despite the churning in her stomach. They all turned to AJ, but he was staring up at the pinnacle of the Viper with a wistful smile on his face. "You guys go ahead," he said. "I'll meet up with you at the snack stand later, all right?"

Without waiting for an answer, he wandered off down the curving concrete path, not even realizing his three friends were staring at his retreating back in stunned surprise.

Chapter Eight

Man it's just da game, I just play it to play it
—Jay-Z

That was, like, the best day ever," Heidi said happily as Kevin pulled off the exit to Santa Barbara. "Yeah, it was a real blast," Ciara said, trying to keep the sarcasm out of her voice. She stared out the front windshield at the neat white houses rising above them on the hills overlooking the ocean. Heidi had "generously" suggested that Ciara ride shotgun because of her stomach, and she'd been giggling and nudging AJ in the backseat all the way home. Even the amazing Hieroglyphics CD Kevin had put on couldn't distract her from the feeling of unrest in the pit of her stomach.

She kept feeling like there were undercurrents of flirtation floating toward them from the backseat, but then she'd sneak a glance in the rearview mirror to find AJ just staring out the window, bobbing his head slightly to the beat. Was something really going on between him and Heidi, or was she just being paranoid?

"So hey," Kevin said, pulling into Heidi's driveway. "I'm spinning on this party boat down at the pier tomorrow night. It should be a good time."

AJ's gorgeous eyes sparkled as he turned to Heidi. "He got me free tickets. Want to come?"

Ciara's cheeks flamed. If AJ wanted to ask Heidi out, that was fine. But did he have to do it right in front of her? The only thing that could have made her feel any worse was if Heidi flung her arms around AJ's neck and kissed his cheek in gratitude. Which was exactly what she did.

"I'd love to!" she shrieked, her voice reaching a pitch Ciara had never heard outside of a Teletubbies cartoon.

"I'll knock you a plus-one too, Ciara," AJ said quickly, probably sensing that she was about to reach into the backseat and strangle Heidi with the drawstring on the hood of her jumper. "We'll all go. It'll be tight."

"Thanks," Ciara said. Kevin gave her a look that seemed to say, *This is our chance,* and she returned it with a subtle nod. She bet she had more experience than

Heidi when it came to grinding on the dance floor—this was clearly a great opportunity to show off her moves.

"Hey, Ciara!" Heidi turned to her. "Want to come to the mall and pick out something to wear? I'm supposed to meet Marlene there in an hour anyway."

The very last thing Ciara wanted to do was watch Heidi try on the skimpiest outfit in every store in the mall. Then again, if this was going to turn into a full-on competition, she needed something to wear too.

"Sure," she heard herself saying. Maybe this would be a chance to pump Heidi for details on what was going on with her and AJ as well.

"Cool!" Heidi chirped. She turned to AJ. "I guess I'll see you tomorrow night." Ciara could actually see her struggling to come up with something cute and clever to say—her brow furrowed for a moment before she gave up and opened the door, hopping lightly to the pavement.

Kevin's car pulled out of the driveway, and Ciara climbed into the passenger seat of Heidi's white Kia Spectra. Heidi turned the key in the ignition, and Jessica Simpson came blasting through the speakers. Ciara winced. In addition to stealing her man, Heidi had really cheesy taste in music.

Heidi nodded along, her shaggy platinum hair fluttering in the breeze from the air conditioner.

"So you had fun today?" Ciara asked.

"Totally," Heidi said. She still had a far-off glimmer in her eye. "Didn't you?"

"Sure," Ciara said. "I actually had a really good time checking out that bluegrass band with Kevin. He knows so much about music, it's amazing."

"Neat," Heidi said. She seemed distracted, a shy grin fluttering across her face as she stared intently at the road. "Look, if I tell you something, do you promise to keep it a secret?"

"Of course," Ciara said. Her palms suddenly felt damp.

"You have to promise," Heidi repeated. "Because I don't want this getting back to Marlene."

"Pinkie swear." Ciara held up her pinkie and raised an eyebrow, but Heidi barely took her eyes off the road. She was obviously concentrating hard on what she was about to confess.

"Okay, cool," she said. She took a deep breath. "I kissed AJ," she said quickly.

"Really?" Ciara asked, trying to sound surprised. Even though she could have guessed it was coming, the news still made her ache.

"Yeah." Heidi looked like she was about to swoon over the wheel. "Right before we got on the Viper."

"Wow," Ciara said. The dampness in her palms was starting to feel slimy. "How was it?"

"Amazing." Heidi sighed. "Ciara, honestly? I thought

I was going to die."

"The Viper will do that to you," Ciara quipped. Just thinking about it made her feel like she'd left her stomach up at the top of Scream!

Heidi laughed a short, nervous laugh. "No, but seriously. He's such an incredible kisser. He has these supersoft lips, and I just felt like I was going to melt into a big puddle all over the roller coaster as soon as he touched me."

"I'm glad you didn't," Ciara said seriously. "It probably would have jammed the gears."

Heidi threw back her head and howled with laughter. "Wow, Ciara, you are hilarious. You know, I'm really glad to have you back. You're, like, the only person I can really talk to about this stuff. I mean, *please* don't tell Marlene. Like, I know they broke up and everything, but she might still be kind of pissed that I hooked up with her ex, you know?"

"My lips are sealed," Ciara assured her.

"Phew!" Heidi pulled into a parking space and cut the engine, but she didn't get out of the car. Instead, she turned and looked at Ciara, a serious expression on her face. "Can I tell you something else?" she asked.

"Sure." Without the air conditioner blasting, the car suddenly felt too hot. Sweat was starting to trickle down the insides of her arms.

Heidi looked down at her hands, which were twisting around each other in her lap. "That was only the second time I ever kissed a guy," she whispered.

Ciara had no idea how to respond. Why was Heidi even telling her this? "Congratulations . . . ?" she said.

"Thanks." Heidi let out a nervous little giggle and peered through the windshield, still avoiding Ciara's gaze. "I feel so dumb. I mean, I'm sixteen. Most of the girls I know have already lost their virginity. I just feel so, like, inexperienced and out of it, and that's kind of why I decided to be a little more wild this summer."

"Seems like it's working," Ciara remarked. Doubt was starting to wrench at her insides. Operation Woo-ha had seemed like a good idea when she saw herself and Heidi as equals, but seeing her as this vulnerable little girl who had only made out with two guys and was turning to her for kissing advice just made it seem . . . wrong. Devious. Well, more devious than it had been in the first place.

"I hope so," Heidi said. "Because the first guy I kissed . . . that didn't turn out so well."

Ciara wondered if she was talking about Jude, but Heidi answered the question before she even had a chance to ask. Her eyes grew wide and dark as she confessed how crazy she'd been about Jude and how hurt and mortified she'd been when he dumped her for the wilder, more experienced Princess. Heidi obviously saw

AJ as her chance for redemption from being dumped—if Heidi the wild child could land AJ, she could land anyone. Which Ciara supposed would be all good except that AJ was supposed to be *her* redemption too!

The curious, wide-eyed stare Heidi was giving her wasn't doing a lot to make her feel better about herself. "Have you kissed a lot of guys?" Heidi asked her point-blank.

A cold bubble of dread rose in Ciara's stomach. How did Heidi *know*?

"I mean—sorry, that came out sounding weird," Heidi continued. "But I mean, you're from LA, and I figure people there are kind of more sophisticated and experienced."

Ciara relaxed. Heidi was actually sort of paying her a compliment.

"I've smooched my fair share," she said cautiously. "It's fun, but nothing to freak out over. Just don't worry that you're doing it wrong and you'll be fine. There's no 'wrong' way to kiss. Chances are, the guy will be so psyched to be kissing you that he won't exactly be critiquing your technique."

She couldn't believe it. Earlier that day she'd been plotting to steal AJ's attention away from Heidi—now she was giving her sisterly advice. How twisted was that?

"All right," Heidi said slowly. "So, like, what does it

mean if he pulls away really quickly? Does that mean he's just not that into you, or whatever?"

"Well, not necessarily," Ciara said. "Sometimes guys get nervous that they're going to get too turned on, and that's why they pull back. Or, like . . . well, something could distract them, or maybe they want to look at you. It's hard to say. Why, did AJ pull back?" The thought of AJ pulling away from Heidi made her feel smug in a way she didn't like but couldn't help. Maybe Heidi didn't have what it took to land a guy like AJ after all.

"Well, it was kind of hard to tell," Heidi admitted. "I mean, three seconds later we were upside down, and it's not exactly easy to make out when you're corkscrewing through the air at sixty miles per hour."

"Then maybe it was that," Ciara said. "It's hard to tell with guys sometimes."

"Cool," Heidi said. Then she started to laugh. "It's so dumb that I need someone to tell me stuff like that. I mean, any magazine would have said the same thing, but somehow . . . I don't know, it's like it feels more authentic coming from you. You know?"

"I guess," Ciara said.

"Have I mentioned how glad I am you're back in town?" Heidi asked.

"I think once or twice." Ciara let her face relax into

a grin. It was nice to have a girlfriend who actually cared if she was around or not. Em was so wrapped up in Tim by the time Ciara had left LA that sometimes she wondered whether her best friend would even notice once she left town. "So do you think things are going to get serious with you and AJ?"

Heidi giggled, and her cheeks glowed pink. "I don't think so. I mean, he just got out of a relationship, and I'm all about getting in touch with my wild side this summer. But I figure, if anyone can bring out the tiger in me, it's AJ. I think we're going to have a lot of fun."

Her giggles snaked right through Ciara's ears and scratched at her heart like nails down a chalkboard. It was so unfair! Of all the people that Heidi could have tagged for her Girl Gone Wild experiment, did it *have* to be AJ? She wished she could tell Heidi to go find someone else to play with because she had plans for AJ that involved more than just casual summer fun. Heidi had gotten to be the "good girl" her whole life, and now that Ciara had decided it was her turn, Heidi was yanking the opportunity right out from under her.

"Anyway, if you can keep it on the DL around Marlene, I'd really appreciate it," Heidi said for the third time, opening the car door and stepping out.

"Don't worry," Ciara said. "You can count on me."

*   *   *

Ciara's phone beeped as they entered the mall. It was a text message from Kevin.

AJ goes nuts for tennis skirts was all it said.

"Who are you texting with?" Heidi wanted to know as they headed toward Smoothie City.

"Just my dad." Ciara rolled her eyes. "He wants to know what I want for dinner."

"That's so sweet," Heidi crooned, spotting Marlene and waving. They made their way across the crowded food court to Smoothie City, where Marlene had perched on one of the stools to drink her Kiwi Dream and peruse the latest issue of *Teen People*.

"Hey!" She closed the magazine and gave them each a hug. "How was Six Flags? Was AJ beating up little kids to get to the front of the line like he always does?"

Ciara laughed. "He was remarkably well-behaved." Out of the corner of her eye, she saw Heidi turn beet red. If she was going to sneak around with her friend's ex, Ciara thought, she'd have to work on that poker face.

"Yeah, it's too bad you couldn't be there to witness it," Heidi said quickly. "Hey, I'm going to go get a smoothie. Want one?"

"No thanks," Ciara said, hopping up on a stool next to Marlene. "I'm still full from those corn dogs."

They watched her get in line and make eye contact

with the guy behind the counter, whose barbed wire tattoo peeked out from under the short sleeve of his purple polyester uniform shirt. Heidi smiled, blushed, and looked down at the floor, twisting a strand of hair around her finger.

Ciara glanced at Marlene, whose russet-colored hair formed a shimmering cloud around her face. She wished she could just come out and ask her point-blank about AJ: what their relationship had been like, why they broke up, and what it was like kissing him and talking to him and calling him her boyfriend. Instead, she turned to Marlene, smiled, and asked, "How was work?"

"All right." Marlene sighed. "I'm a little annoyed—they told me when they hired me that I'd actually learn how to cut and color hair, but all they have me doing is sweeping the floor and telling these little old ladies which chair to sit in. It's kind of disappointing."

"Bummer," Ciara said sympathetically. She wondered if there was some way she could bring AJ into the conversation without sounding completely obvious.

"So how were the roller coasters?" Marlene asked. "I haven't even been to Six Flags yet this season, and I'm dying to give Tatsu a test run. Honestly, I might have even tried to take off work, but Heidi said she wasn't sure if you guys were really going to go."

Ciara was too shocked to say anything. When Heidi

had invited her the day before, she'd made it sound like
the trip was definitely on. Had she been deliberately trying to keep Marlene away for the day? That was pretty
sneaky. And then she remembered her own relief that
very morning when she'd learned that Marlene wasn't
coming and started to feel a little icky inside.

"Were the lines long?" Marlene asked, trying to prod
Ciara out of her silence. "Did you get to go on a lot of
rides?"

"Actually, not so much," Ciara confessed. She told
Marlene about feeling sick after Scream! and how Kevin
had stayed on the ground.

"Kevin's sweet like that," Marlene said. "He was
really there for me when AJ and I broke up."

Ciara couldn't believe her luck. She didn't even need to
rack her brain trying to come up with ways to work AJ into
the conversation—Marlene had dropped it right in her lap.

"That must have been rough," she said. "Why did
you guys split?"

Marlene sighed and took a long sip of her smoothie.
"The whole band thing really got in the way," she said.
"As soon as they started playing out and getting fans,
AJ's ego got way too big for his head. I kept being like,
'Dude, remember you're still human and so am I and
you have to respect that,' but he was off in his own
little world."

"So you dumped him?" Ciara asked, trying not to sound incredulous. Marlene had always seemed pretty sane to her, but what girl in her right mind would dump AJ? If AJ was *her* boyfriend, she would do whatever it took to keep him around.

"Sort of," Marlene said. "I mean, it was kind of mutual. Or more, like, I broke up with him, but he didn't exactly beg me to reconsider. He kind of felt like the relationship was getting in the way of his never-ending quest for stardom or whatever."

Ciara wondered if she could ask Marlene if she still missed him, but it was too late. Heidi was bouncing up to them, an extra-large smoothie in one hand and a huge grin on her face.

"Guess what?" she said, hopping onto the stool next to Ciara.

"What?" Ciara and Marlene chorused dutifully.

"That guy at the counter?" Heidi was trying to keep her voice down, but excitement crept into it nonetheless. "He totally gave me a free smoothie in exchange for my e-mail!"

"Uh, Heidi?" Marlene said. "You know that's, like, the cheesiest line in the history of human interpersonal relations, right? Please tell me you didn't fall for it."

Heidi blushed like it was about to go out of style. "He was cute . . . ," she protested.

"Yeah, that nineties-boy-band-reject tattoo really got me going too," Marlene said sarcastically. Heidi looked like she was about to pout but decided to start giggling instead.

Ciara looked down at her sneakers, not sure what to say. All she could think was that if Heidi was willing to flirt with any sleazeball behind the counter of a smoothie bar at the mall, she definitely didn't deserve AJ. Any lingering doubts about Operation Woo-ha melted away. Heidi was obviously just going after anything with a Y chromosome. What would she care if Ciara ended up with AJ? She'd be too busy flirting with the next guy who offered her a free cup of pureed berries to even notice.

"You're so mean!" Heidi joked, punching Marlene lightly on the arm. "So what if I want to flirt with the guy at the smoothie bar? We can't all be super-long-term-relationship-only girls like you. Some of us just want to have fun."

She looked at Ciara for backup. *Speak for yourself,* Ciara wanted to say, but she'd felt the same way—oh, two whole weeks ago. "It's true," she agreed, looking at both Heidi and Marlene. "Now, are we going to sit here arguing boy semantics all night, or are we going to hit some stores?"

Chapter Nine

You think you're cute, you think you're fine
You're always trying to steal my shine
—Destiny's Child

Dusk was setting in, and the last pink streaks of sunset faded from the sky as Ciara approached the pier where the party boat was docked. The tangy scent of the ocean wafted toward her from the waves gently lapping the pilings below, and she breathed in deeply, letting the warm night breeze caress her bare legs and flutter her hair over her shoulders.

The weathered wooden shops along the pier were decorated in tiny, twinkling white Christmas lights, and the boat glowed like a jack-o'-lantern bobbing on the water, each of its portholes ablaze with lights. She could see lines of colorful lanterns strung along the top deck and hear the faint thudding of bass. As she made her way along the pier, she passed small groups talking and laughing as they ambled toward the boat. Sequins sparkled from filmy peasant blouses, and rhinestones twinkled from the back pockets of tight, low-rise, well-distressed jeans. The air on the pier seemed alive and buzzing with the possibility that lay in the night ahead: a four-hour cruise with bumping tunes and the hottest dance floor south of San Francisco.

Ciara spotted a platinum-blond head bobbing through the crowd ahead of her and hurried to catch up. She threw an arm over Heidi's shoulders, and Heidi looked up at her with wide, surprised eyes before breaking into a relieved smile.

"Hey, Ciara!" she cried, wrapping her arm around Ciara's waist. "I am *so psyched* for tonight! Aren't you?"

Heidi had poured herself into a teal bouclé Zara minidress with satin ribbons decorating the low neckline and layers of ruffles along the hem. Her eyes were lined with heavy black kohl, her lids shadowed to match the dress. It gave her eyes a vampy, salacious look that seemed like an odd contrast with her bubbly personality and round, innocent-looking face.

"Should be a good time," Ciara said.

Heidi disentangled herself and stood back to get a look at Ciara's outfit. "Wow," she said. "White pleated miniskirt? I never really thought of that as your style."

Ciara shrugged. "I wanted to wear something comfortable so I could dance, and this was on sale." Yeah, right. If you considered eighty-five dollars *on sale*. She had never spent so much money on what essentially amounted to a loincloth in her life, but Kevin had assured her when she called him back from the mall's bathroom that AJ had once spent twenty minutes going off on how hot miniskirts looked on girls with nice legs, so somehow the skirt seemed worth it. She'd paired it with a simple black tank decorated with beads and lace and her favorite Steve Madden espadrilles—the ones she could walk *and* dance in. She was dressed to impress one person: AJ. If piquing his interest with her style and moves on the dance floor didn't work, she didn't know what would.

"Well, you look like you could out-Kournikova Kournikova," Heidi said.

Ciara was bowled over by the compliment. Why did Heidi have to go and be so nice? She felt like she'd been socked in the stomach with a heavy dose of Woo-ha guilt.

"You look pretty hot yourself," Ciara said.

"Really?" Heidi asked, chewing the ragged edge of

her thumbnail. "Do you think AJ will like it? Is it wild enough? Everyone here looks so hip." She looked around at the groups of girls streaming toward the boat, her mouth twisted with worry.

Despite her irritation at the AJ comment, Ciara's heart went out to Heidi. She seemed so young and inexperienced, like a little girl playing dress-up in her mother's closet. This wasn't the false bravado she showed around boys. It was just Heidi trying a personality makeover that might or might not be working.

"Don't worry about it," she said, giving Heidi's arm a squeeze. "You look like you're here to have fun. Isn't that what this is all about?"

Heidi shot her a grateful smile as they approached the boat and saw AJ and Kevin standing by the gangway. Pangs of longing shot through her at the sight of AJ, whose biceps bulged enticingly from a sleeveless Lakers jersey. They all hugged hello, and as Ciara buried her head in AJ's neck and his arms wrapped briefly around her, she breathed in his sexy scent and never wanted to let go.

"Damn, Ciara," AJ said, holding her at arm's length as they pulled away. "That skirt is *smokin'*!"

Heidi threw her a questioning look, and Kevin winked at her over AJ's shoulder, but all she did was smile and say thanks. Score one for Ciara! She could feel AJ's eyes on her even as he hugged Heidi, and her head swam with a feeling of triumph. Tonight was the night. She was going to make it *happen*. And as for Heidi . . . well, a million other guys were here. Including Kevin, who was in the middle of telling everyone that the boat had a really great grill in case anyone was hungry.

"I'm hungrier than Nicole Richie on a ten-day juice fast," AJ said, and they all laughed.

Kevin led the way past the line that had formed on the ship's gangway and approached a bouncer approximately the size of two football players put together. "Hey, O-Man," Kevin said. "These are my plus ones."

O-Man nodded once, and a woman in a slinky black dress attached red bands to their wrists. The bands said UNDER 21 in bold black letters.

"This totally clashes with my outfit," Heidi quipped, looking at the band.

"Outfit?" AJ joked. "What this clashes with is my plans to get wasted!"

"Chill, celebutante," Ciara said, rolling her eyes. She hoped the bouncer would realize AJ was just kidding. Kevin had already warned them that if they so much as looked longingly at a beer, they risked getting him kicked off the job.

She and Heidi stuck close to AJ as Kevin led them through a pair of swinging doors and into the boat's restaurant, where rough-hewn wooden tables were nailed into the floor beneath large, round portholes overlooking the ocean and the twinkling lights of the pier.

"This is the best time to come," Kevin explained as he led them to a table, where Heidi quickly slipped in next to AJ, leaving Ciara to sit side by side with Kevin. Oh, well, at least she was opposite AJ so they could make eye contact throughout the meal. "Everyone goes up to the deck to watch the boat leave the pier, and then as soon as it does, they all decide they're hungry and come down here and the place is mobbed and you can't get a table."

"Wow, you really know your way around this boat," Ciara said, trying to talk Kevin up in front of Heidi the way they'd planned.

"Well, I've spun here a few times," Kevin said modestly. "It's an amazing gig—usually they get college students, but I got lucky. The dude who books this thing likes to root around on the Internet for unknown local talent."

A foghorn sounded, and Ciara looked out the window just in time to see the boat slowly pulling away from the pier. Cheers sounded from the open deck above.

"Yay, we're moving!" Heidi shouted happily. Ciara felt the energy from the boat's forward motion surge through her as she joined the rest of the table in clapping and cheering. They were off the mainland, on the water and headed for adventure. Across the table, AJ's eyes caught hers and held them for one heart-stopping moment before the waitress appeared.

"What can I get you guys?" she asked.

Ciara had barely had time to look at the menu. She quickly scanned it and ordered a veggie burger—the protein would give her extra energy to dance all night.

"I'll have the Caesar salad," Heidi said. "And a Diet Coke."

"Chicken?" the waitress asked.

"No!" Heidi looked shocked, and the rest of the table laughed. She'd been a strict vegetarian for as long as they'd all known her. In fact, she was so passionate about animal rights, she wouldn't even wear real leather shoes.

Which was why, when AJ ordered a bacon cheeseburger extra rare, they all looked at Heidi, expecting her to launch into another one of her lectures about the mistreatment of cows on the huge commercial ranches in the Midwest. But Heidi stared at AJ with lovesick puppy eyes, as if he'd just announced the cure for cancer instead of ordering a giant slab of bloody bovine.

"You know, AJ, a cow had to give up its life so you could have that burger," Kevin reprimanded him when the waitress had gone.

"Animals, please." AJ laughed. "I need energy food—I'm going to hit the dance floor like it's never been hit tonight." He looked happier than Ciara had ever seen him besides when he was onstage, and she wondered if it had anything to do with the way he'd looked at her when he'd first seen her dressed up for the cruise. Was it just her imagination, or had he kept sneaking glances her way ever since they'd sat down?

"Me too." Heidi sighed dreamily, staring at AJ as she sipped her Diet Coke.

Ciara looked at Kevin and felt her eyes rolling way up in their sockets, almost like she couldn't control them. It sucked to see someone compromise herself so much over a boy—especially when that boy happened to be someone *she* wanted.

"So." AJ was leaning across the table, his wide-set eyes gleaming with excitement. "I've got some killer news."

"What?" Heidi and Ciara asked simultaneously.

AJ's eyes twinkled, and his broad shoulders seemed to widen even more with the news he was about to spill. He looked straight at Kevin. "We're opening for the Coup when they play the Velvet Lounge at the end of August!"

"What?!" Kevin almost dropped his root beer all over the table. "Dude, this is *huge*! Why didn't you tell me sooner?"

"I wanted it to be a surprise." AJ grinned deviously. "I figured if I told you right before your set, you'd really spin some pumping tunes."

"Wow." Kevin was fidgeting in his seat like a nervous middle-school girl on her first date. "That's completely amazing. They're only, like, the best thing to come out of Oakland *ever*."

"I love the Coup," Ciara broke in. Only a guy with AJ's drive and passion would be able to land a gig like that! She figured it was time to impress him with her musical knowledge. "Their songs have such incredible narrative. Like, 'Me and Jesus the Pimp in a '79 Granada.' When you listen to it, there are all these hidden messages, but it just sounds like they're telling a story."

"It's a lot to live up to," Kevin agreed.

AJ was still looking at Ciara, nodding and smiling. "But if anyone can live up to them, it's the B-Dizzy Crew."

"Maybe you should let me be your backup dancer," Heidi suggested, scooting closer to AJ on the bench.

"Sure," AJ joked, casually draping an arm over her shoulders. "As long as you wear a thong and go-go boots like the dancers in Twista's video."

Ciara snuck an annoyed glance at Kevin. His mouth was slightly open and he had a faraway look in his eyes, possibly at the thought of their upcoming gig, but maybe at the image AJ had just painted. Not that Heidi wore much more than that on a daily basis anyway, Ciara thought angrily. Why did Heidi have to keep stealing the spotlight with her cute-girl act? It had taken Ciara years to accumulate all her hip-hop knowledge, but Heidi had cut right through that with her new "wild girl" thing.

She reminded herself not to sulk as their food came, and she dug into her veggie burger. But when she looked up to see Heidi gazing adoringly at AJ, who was tearing into his cheeseburger so vigorously that a thin line of meat juice ran down the corner of his mouth, she had to struggle to repress the resentment that rose in her throat. She tried to remind herself that no matter what happened, they were all just here to have fun. It was summer, it was a beautiful night, and they were at Santa Barbara's hottest movable party—for free! But none of those thoughts seemed to help. AJ loomed before her, chewing his burger and laughing at something Heidi had said, and he was all that mattered. Wanting him had taken over her life so thoroughly that it seemed like it was in her blood— her heartbeat repeated his name each time it thudded in her chest: *A.-J. A.-J. A.-J.*

"Hey, I have to get going," Kevin said, interrupting her thoughts as he slurped up the last of his root beer. "My set starts in twenty minutes."

Ciara suddenly felt very uncomfortable. Operation Woo-ha was one thing when Kevin was around, but when it was just her versus Heidi, it felt like some kind of covert, catty gladiator battle. AJ smiled and stretched his hands over his head.

"Have fun," he said. "I'll wave to you from the dance floor."

"Spin some Pussycat Dolls for me!" Heidi called after him. Ciara winced. Why did Heidi have to have such generic taste in music? She caught AJ's eye and they shared a conspiratorial gaze that gave her confidence a momentary surge. In the music category, she definitely had Heidi pinned to the floor. But then there was everything else . . .

"I can't wait to shake my tail feather!" Heidi was already bouncing up and down in her seat to the bass thumping from the deck above.

"Let's do it," AJ agreed. They paid the bill and rose from the table, threading their way through the boat's crowded restaurant (Kevin had been right about everyone rushing down after the launch), past all the groups of girls in tiny tank tops and guys with wind-tousled hair drinking and laughing like they were having the best time in the world. Ciara was determined to look as overjoyed to be on the party boat as they were. This was her chance to impress AJ with her fun-loving attitude and great moves on the dance floor. If she couldn't upstage Heidi tonight, she might not have the chance again.

"This is so much fun!" she said, pushing between AJ and Heidi and grabbing each of their arms. She smiled madly, so wide that it hurt her face, and tried to match her voice to Heidi's light, bubbly enthusiasm.

AJ gave her a funny look with a raised eyebrow. She knew her tone sounded a little forced—she was usually much more laid-back, the kind of girl who could say more with a half smile than by shouting and jumping up and down. This bubbly stuff was so not her territory, but given what she'd seen of Heidi, it seemed to be what he responded to. It felt strange trying to act like someone she wasn't, and she wasn't entirely sure she was comfortable with it. But what did it matter? She could go back to being herself as soon as she and AJ were officially together.

Up on the main deck, the dance floor looked like a giant amoeba gliding back and forth to the beat, the occasional raised hand flailing out and above the sea of heads like an errant tentacle. The ocean air energized the mass of bodies, and the colored lights strung from high poles around the deck played against the water below, flickering and gleaming like secrets rising from the dark depths.

Ciara looked up at the DJ booth, where a girl with

blond dreads was handing the headphones over to Kevin. He gave her a quick peck on the cheek before turning to riffle through his record bag, and she came trotting down the narrow metal stairs to the dance floor.

Kevin seemed to have found what he was looking for. He held the record up for a moment before flipping it onto the turntable and hunching over it, moving it back and forth with one hand to cue it up. He flicked some switches on the mixer and a strong, sultry beat came booming through the fade-out on the previous song.

"Yeah!" The dance floor seemed to scream as one voice. Dozens of fists pumped the air. The beat dropped like a firebomb into the sea of gyrating butts and swiveling hips, and Ciara felt it moving her as well, the energy from the bodies flowing all around her, filling her up so that the music zipped through her limbs. She felt like her body would explode if she didn't start dancing.

Still holding AJ and Heidi by the arms, she began to snake her way through the crowd to the middle of the dance floor.

"This good?" Ciara shouted to AJ and Heidi over the music. She'd found a small spot in the dead center of the dance floor, with a surplus of guys around in case Heidi decided she wanted to go for one of them instead of AJ—which, given the Smoothie City incident the day before, wasn't a total long shot. But instead of disappearing into the cluster of guys as Ciara had hoped, Heidi began dancing right in front of AJ, lowering her head and gazing up at him mischievously from below her heavily painted lashes. Her moves got bolder as she edged toward him, circling her butt like a terrier in heat. Ciara noted with annoyance that Heidi wasn't nearly as good a dancer as she was. Heidi could barely keep the beat—all she did was, as she herself had said earlier, "shake her tail feather."

Plus, Ciara was left with nobody to dance with. She glanced up at AJ, hoping he would see the pleading look in her eyes, but his face was buried in Heidi's hair as his large, strong hands guided her hips against his. Ciara could have puked—they were grinding right in front of her, as if she wasn't even there. She looked around wildly and saw the group of guys she'd landed in the midst of, their eyes red in the theatrical lights, circling the dance floor, their teeth gleaming, mouths open like hungry wolves. She tried telling herself not to freak out—once upon a time two weeks ago, she would have been happy for the attention. She would have picked one of the guys out of the crowd and motioned with her eyes for him to approach her, savoring the buildup as their bodies circled each other before connecting. And then she'd be left with that cold, empty feeling in her gut once again, that feeling that embodied everything about her old life in LA she wanted to leave behind. She wasn't going to fall back into being the queen of meaningless hookups again. She was going to make AJ see that they were meant to be together, and everything would be fine.

But as she looked past the circle of heads to AJ, envy lodged in her gut. He was leaning close to Heidi, whispering something in her ear as she threw back her head in laughter. Ciara began to push through the crowd, still half consciously moving with the beat. She didn't know what she was looking for, only that seeing the one thing she wanted more than anything else in the world yanked away from her was too painful to watch. And it was true—somehow in the last three days, she'd dived headlong into a major crush on AJ. She couldn't explain it, but she just felt like it was the right thing—maybe the only thing at all. . . .

The crowd became a sea of sparkling tank tops and flailing elbows. She heard a girl laughing drunkenly by her left ear and saw her long yellow hair swing back and forth as she stumbled about the dance floor, balancing precariously on tall Lucite heels. Red wine sloshed back and forth in the glass she held in front of her. She reached for a guy who was pushing through the crowd ahead of Ciara, lurched suddenly to the side, and bumped sharply against Ciara's hip.

"Whoops," she slurred.

"Watch your glass!" Ciara cried.

But it was too late. Red wine cascaded from the glass, and Ciara couldn't jump out of the way in time. The wine spilled onto her, making a dark, ugly stain the shape of the Hawaiian Islands down the front of Ciara's brand-new, eighty-five-dollar, bought-for-the-sole-purpose-of-impressing-AJ bright white teeny-tiny tennis skirt.

Chapter Ten

When the female and male come in contact
Sticky situation in fact
Tryin' not to let the feelings catch

—Jurassic 5

Ciara fought her way through the mass of revelers to the bar, trying to keep the tears that stung her eyes from spilling over onto her cheeks. She held her hands down by her sides and shouldered her way through the sea of gyrating pelvises and waving arms, muttering "excuse me" as she jostled past.

The crowd at the bar was three deep. Guys with hair gelled up into points at the top of their heads like Kewpie dolls waved twenty-dollar bills as their fake-tanned girlfriends clung impatiently to their sides. Everyone was vying for the attention of two sharp-featured bartenders with their hair pulled back in slick, gleaming ponytails, who took money and poured drinks with the quick, precise movements of hawks stalking their prey.

It took what felt like aeons for Ciara to edge in close enough to catch the attention of the skinnier bartender, and during that time, she felt the wine soaking through her skirt and into her skin. The bartender's slim, straight nose wrinkled in disgust when she asked for a club soda, no lime.

"Four dollars," she snarled, slamming the drink down so that it sloshed onto the pitted wood.

Four dollars for a glass of bubbly water? Ciara sighed, handed her a five, and grabbed a handful of cocktail napkins before slinking away to an empty spot near the railing overlooking the dark, swirling ocean below. She wished she could just dive overboard and swim back to shore, but the lights of Santa Barbara twinkled like a toy village in a model train exhibit way in the distance.

She dipped a cocktail napkin in the club soda and began dabbing miserably at the blood-colored stain on her skirt. It would look to anyone else like she'd gotten her period at a very unfortunate time, and the wine had soaked so deeply into the flimsy material that the club soda wasn't making much of a difference.

Next to her, a couple cooed at each other from the dark recesses of a locked embrace, reminding her of what a failure Operation Woo-ha was turning out to be. She looked over the rail again, at the black surface of the water rolling gently under them. If she just jumped in, she would never have to go back to LA and the mess she'd made of her life there again. She could sink below the surface, and AJ would spend the rest of his life wondering what could have been between them if only he'd paid attention to her instead of Heidi that fateful night on the party boat. He'd write song after song dedicated to her, and Em would realize she should have spent more time with her and less with her stupid boyfriend, and her mom would regret ever having broken up the family. . . .

She knew she was being melodramatic. To distract herself from her morbid thoughts, Ciara looked up at the DJ booth. Kevin had the headphones over one ear and was biting his lower lip in concentration. She watched as he made the transition from one track to the next, then rested the headphones on his neck and scanned the crowd. He nodded in approval at the packed dance floor before moving his eyes over the bar, down the rail past Ciara, and then quickly back again. Seeing her standing by herself, he pantomimed an elaborate shrug, as if to say, *What's going on?*

Ciara grimaced back at him and then pointed to her

skirt. A look of almost-comic alarm crossed his face, and Kevin quickly motioned for her to join him in the DJ booth. She nodded before taking a deep breath and forcing her way back through the crowd. This time, she kept her hands clasped self-consciously in front of the stain, which made elbowing past the writhing bodies even more difficult.

"Watch it!" she heard a girl shout as she struggled past, but she was already on to the next knot of dancers. Kevin had dropped a new track by the time she reached the narrow metal staircase leading to the DJ booth. Ciara suddenly realized she would have to climb it, putting her higher than almost everyone else on the boat, with a giant red stain on her crotch. She contemplated the stairs for a while, then turned so that her butt faced the crowd and climbed up sideways, like a crab. It crossed her mind that she probably looked even more moronic than she would have if she'd just climbed the stairs normally, but it was too late. She was already in the DJ booth, her back still to the crowd as she pretended to be fascinated by Kevin's messy record bag sitting on a chair behind the turntables.

Kevin placed a concerned hand on her shoulder. "What happened?"

"A drunk girl spilled wine on my skirt," Ciara said. "Do you have any idea how much this thing cost?"

"It can't have been that much," Kevin said. "I mean, it's got to be like six square inches of fabric at the most."

"Don't you know the cardinal rule of summer couture?" Ciara asked bitterly. "The smaller the garment, the bigger the price tag."

"Guess I'm behind on my women's fashion," Kevin quipped, crouching down and rummaging beneath the chair on which his record bag sat. He emerged with a large navy blue Adidas windbreaker. "It gets cold here sometimes at night, so I usually bring a jacket. It should be long enough on you to cover up the stain."

"Thanks!" It seemed like Kevin was always saving her butt these days. First he'd stayed on the ground with her at Six Flags, and now this. She snuggled into the light, fleece-lined jacket as he flipped through the LPs in his record bag. It came down lower than the hem of the skirt and smelled like Tide and old records, just like him.

"I don't think that look will make it to the runways this season," Kevin observed. "But it does the job." He turned and placed the record on one of the turntables, holding up a finger to let her know to hang on while he cued it up.

Ciara looked down at the crowd. From up in the DJ booth, she had a panoramic view of the dance floor, the bar, and the stairs leading down to the lower levels. It was obviously the best seat in the house, and being up there with Kevin was safe and relaxing, like they were two kids hiding out in a tree fort. Instead of a hungry amoeba eager to swallow her into its yawning maw, the dance floor looked like a sea of bobble heads attached to small, delicate bodies. She could see the parts in everyone's hair and the glowing tips of cigarettes, the occasional beaded shirt catching the colored spotlights and winking up at her.

Suddenly, her eyes zeroed in on a pair of heads in the center of the dance floor: a perfectly round, brown skull with a close-cropped coating of black fuzz and, much farther down, Heidi's shaggy platinum locks. As Ciara stared, transfixed, Heidi straddled AJ's leg, grinding her pelvis suggestively. AJ's hands roamed up and down her back, lingering on her butt and drawing it closer to him. Ciara could literally feel her blood pressure rise as Heidi stared up at him, her eyes glittering rapturously, for a long moment before she buried her face in his neck.

"What's wrong?" Kevin asked. She must have looked as frustrated and disgusted as she felt. She pointed wordlessly toward the human knot AJ and Heidi had formed with their bodies.

"Oh." Kevin sighed.

Ciara slumped against the railing, her hands dangling over the boatload of laughing, dancing mass below. The cutest guy on the dance floor was practically lip-locked with her friend, and she felt her confidence seeping away like dishwater down a drain. She was just some loser in a stained skirt she'd paid too much money for, watching helplessly as the only guy she wanted got cozy with someone else.

"Sucks to be us," Kevin said glumly, echoing her thoughts. "I mean, I can move a whole dance floor, but I can't even get a girl to tear her eyes away from AJ long enough to look at me."

"Come on," Ciara said, suddenly feeling the need to comfort him. She turned to look at Kevin. With the headphones resting in sleek silver relief against his neck and his face cast in black and purple shadows from the lights, he looked like an image in a music video: fierce, sleek, and cool. "Heidi just doesn't realize how great you are."

"I'm obviously not *that* great," Kevin protested.

"Yes, you are," Ciara argued. "As far as I'm concerned, you're the best thing that's happened to me all summer."

Kevin's lips loosened into a smile at her praise, and he suddenly seemed very large and very masculine beside her. "Thanks," he said.

As their eyes locked, Ciara felt a tingly sensation bubble up inside her. She gathered the feeling around herself like Kevin's soft, warm windbreaker, luxuriating in it as it protected her from the cool ocean air and the feelings of hurt and regret about Heidi and AJ. Kevin's lips were inches from hers. His eyes flickered with confusion and desire.

The record segued into a long, floating instrumental break that sounded like foghorns and mermaids. Below them, the bobble heads paused mid-bobble, so that the entire dance floor seemed suspended in midair, waiting for the beat to drop.

"Crap!" Kevin suddenly turned from her, shattering the moment into smithereens. He grabbed his headphones and shoved them haphazardly over his ears, leaping toward the mixer and frantically throwing switches and turning dials. She could feel the tension between them wilting like a bad perm on an August day. Kevin placed the needle on the record and squinted in concentration as he moved it back and forth in the groove, looking for the right spot. Biting his lip, he nodded along with the music, suddenly flicking the fader all the way to the right.

The beat dropped and the crowd landed on the dance floor with it, shaking their fists in the air, rocking the boat, and screaming. In their midst, she could see Heidi standing on tiptoe to plant a kiss on AJ's lips.

Kevin turned to her, a shaky smile faltering on his face. "Whoa," he said.

"Yeah," Ciara agreed. She couldn't believe she and Kevin had come so close to kissing. She forced a small laugh that sounded more like a bark. "What was *that*?"

"I was *this* close to train-wrecking," Kevin said, holding his thumb and forefinger millimeters apart.

"Oh." Ciara's voice sounded hollow even though she was shouting to be heard over the music. She hadn't been talking about the music.

"My gig here would have been over for good if I did," Kevin explained. "We're ten minutes away from docking. This is the part of the night people will remember. If I left them with silence to dance to, I'd be royally screwed."

"Oh." She felt like a broken record, uttering the same dumb syllable over and over again, but she didn't know what else to say. What had just *happened*? One moment they'd been mooning over AJ and Heidi, and the next they'd practically been kissing. *That* wasn't supposed to happen. It certainly wasn't part of Operation Woo-ha.

"Anyway, listen," Kevin said, suddenly not meeting her eyes. "I have to clean up a little here, get my vinyl together."

"Oh." Third time in a row. "Okay, then. See you later."

She scurried down the narrow metal stairs toward the throng of exuberant dancers below, no longer cool enough to stand above them and watch. Once again, she was just part of the crowd.

Chapter Eleven

This old boat she's just sitting in the moonlight
Catching the gleam in her eye . . .
Shimmer glimmer I think I'm gonna fall—what?
Catch me mama that's all

—50 Cent

Ciara tried to battle the creeping feeling of weirdness as she approached the dilapidated seaside diner where Kevin had instructed her in a text message that morning to meet him. She still felt unsettled from their encounter on the party boat the night before. After she left the DJ booth, she had stood silently by the railing overlooking the sea, watching the lights from Santa Barbara grow closer and closer as they approached shore. Her insides were a mess, battling between hurt over AJ and confusion about her near kiss with Kevin. If she didn't want him, why had she leaned in like that? That was the kind of thing the old Ciara would have done, and the feeling of having let herself down was unsettling. She could almost feel the slimy post-hookup tendrils swirling in her stomach as she realized how close she'd come to throwing away a picture-perfect romance with AJ just because she felt let down and Kevin had been standing right there. Making AJ her boyfriend was the most important thing in the world: once she had a real relationship, she'd be able to truly start life as the new, better Ciara she was trying to be. How could she have let her goal slip away?

The moment the boat docked, she had fled down the gangplank and run across the boardwalk to her car. The last thing she had wanted was to see AJ, Heidi, or (least of all) Kevin. All she wanted was to go home, take off the vile skirt, crawl into bed, and forget the whole thing had ever happened.

Of course, she was still wearing Kevin's windbreaker. And the next morning, he sent her a text saying he needed it back, which seemed a little strange since the weather for the next week was supposed to be in the nineties. Then again, maybe something had happened after she'd run off the boat and he had more news about Operation Woo-ha. Whatever it was that made him want to see her again so soon, she hoped it didn't have anything to do with their almost kiss from the night before.

A white clapboard shack perched precariously on a rotting wooden dock, the diner had smudgy windows overlooking the rows of canoes, paddleboats, and kayaks bobbing gently in the water. A cracked, peeling wooden sign reading THE BOATHOUSE hung on rusted chains over the door.

Kevin was already seated at one of the booths, his head buried in a book. The inside of the diner was surprisingly cozy. Cheery vases of daisies adorned the vinyl tops of the booths, and a fifties-style jukebox gleamed in the corner.

"What're you reading?" Ciara asked, sliding into the seat across from him.

"Nothing," Kevin said, quickly closing the book and placing it next to him on the seat. Leaning over the table, Ciara craned her neck to get a look at the title.

"The Star Wars Companion?!" She gasped, trying to suppress a laugh. She put her hand over her mouth but ended up snorting around it. "Guess you're not completely over your dorkiness after all."

"Hey, you can take the boy out of the galaxy, but you can't take the galaxy out of the boy," Kevin joked.

"I may not be playing with lightsabers anymore, but I'll always have a little Skywalker in here." He tapped his chest, and Ciara dissolved in giggles. The reference to his former Star Wars obsession was somehow enough to eradicate any awkward "about last night" discussions. Besides, here in the brightly lit diner, they were obviously still cool.

"This place is cute," Ciara observed, looking around the diner.

"I love it here," Kevin admitted. "My parents used to take me here every Wednesday when I was a kid. It was like a family tradition."

He frowned slightly as he said that but quickly brightened when a matronly waitress with an enormous tea-colored bouffant bustled over to take their order. "Hi, Sheila," Kevin said. He introduced her to Ciara, and Sheila smiled warmly.

"I've known Kevin since he was *this big*," she said, holding her hand about a foot off the tabletop.

"Sheila's been working here as long as I can remember," Kevin elaborated after she had taken their order and disappeared behind the swinging wood doors leading to the kitchen. "She's almost like my second mom."

The mention of moms made Ciara scowl. Hers had left a message on her voice mail while she was on the party boat, saying simply that she missed her. It was the last thing Ciara wanted to hear. Thinking about her mom made her think about all the other bad stuff she had left behind in LA—stuff she definitely didn't want to dwell on. It was time to get back to landing the perfect boyfriend right here in Santa Barbara.

"So about Operation Woo-ha," Ciara said. "Are we still on?"

"I think so," Kevin said, leaning toward her across the table. "AJ and I went to Denny's after the party boat last night and I drilled him about his dance floor grinding routine with Heidi. The way he told it, he made it sound like they were just goofing around."

"What else did he say?" Ciara asked eagerly.

Kevin sighed. "Not much to report on the Woo-ha front. But he did mention that you looked really cute in that skirt and he was surprised when you suddenly disappeared from the dance floor. Mostly he just wanted to talk about the set list for the Coup show."

"Sounds like AJ," Ciara said. "I love that his music means so much to him. It's like I've finally met someone as passionate about achieving his goals as I am. We'd be so perfect together . . . if only he'd realize it."

"Hey, that's what I'm here for, right?" Kevin reminded her. "Trust me, I'm talking up Ciara the hip-hop freak slash music-marketing whiz every chance I get."

"You're awesome," Ciara said. Just knowing she had

Kevin on her side made her feel safer and more positive, like she really could make everything work out despite all the setbacks the night before. "And trust me, Heidi's going to get an earful about your amazing DJ skills the next time I see her."

"Woo-ha!" Kevin whooped. At that moment, their food arrived and they busied themselves with scarfing down the fluffiest scrambled eggs, crispiest bacon, and greasiest hash browns Ciara had ever eaten. When she was finished, she stood up and wandered over to the jukebox, and flipped through the CDs. She was expecting more of the old doo-wop and rock that had been playing ever since she'd entered the diner but was surprised to find a variety of musical genres, even hip-hop.

In a compilation CD titled *Rap Hits from the '90s*, she found Big Pun's "Still Not a Player." On a whim, she reached into her pocket, found a quarter, and selected the number for the song. The first chords were belting out over the juke's tinny speakers as she returned to her seat.

"Big Pun?" Kevin asked as she sat back down.

She nodded.

"Haven't heard *this* song in a while."

Ciara shrugged. "They were playing it on the radio a lot for some reason. I've been kind of into it lately."

"Trying to stop being a player?" Kevin joked. Ciara

felt her hands go cold and clammy, but she kept her tone of voice light.

"Nah. Just like the song."

"That's cool." Kevin shrugged.

"Player no mo-o-ore!" sang the jukebox.

Player no more, thought Ciara. That's what Operation Woo-ha was really about to her. Once she had AJ, she could truly stop being a player forever. She stared out at the boats rocking gently on the small waves lapping the dilapidated dock, remembering when her dad used to take her kayaking in the bay. Those were some of the happiest afternoons of her life—just her and her dad out on the ocean. With the right person, it could even be romantic. . . .

"Hey!" she cried suddenly. "I have an idea for Operation Woo-ha. Have you ever been kayaking before?"

"No . . . ," Kevin said slowly.

"Does the idea of being alone in a boat with Heidi appeal to you?"

"Um . . . duh?" Kevin asked.

"Yeah, that's what I'm talking about," Ciara said. "See where I'm going?"

"Not really," Kevin admitted.

"Okay, let me break it down." Her gestures became more animated, the way they always did when she formulated a good idea. "I'm an expert kayaker. It's not that hard—I could teach you the basics. Then we lure AJ and Heidi out here, get them alone with us in the boats—since, after all, we *are* more experienced—and work our magic."

Kevin's eyes gleamed. "I've actually always wanted to learn how to kayak. It looks really cool."

"Well, come on." Ciara was already digging money out of her pocket to pay the bill. "Your first lesson starts in ten minutes!"

*   *   *

Later that afternoon, they were back at the dock, this time with AJ and Heidi in tow. Ciara had changed into a pair of newly cut off cutoffs (extra short for AJ's benefit) and a skimpy green jungle-print bikini top, and she was feeling lively and confident. She had already rented a pair of two-person sea kayaks, which bobbed gently in the water at their feet.

"You really want me to go in a boat with no motor?" AJ asked skeptically. His shoulders bent inward, and he looked nervous. "Isn't that dangerous?"

"Kevin and I are both experienced kayakers," Ciara assured him. She was only stretching the truth slightly—after all, she had given Kevin his first lesson earlier that day. That counted as experience, right? "Stick with us and you'll be fine."

"Although . . ." Kevin trailed off like he was manufacturing a thought for the first time. As if he and Ciara hadn't already rehearsed what they were going to say. "You know, since we're both experienced and neither of you are, it might make sense to put one of us in each boat. Like, Heidi could come with me. And AJ, you could go with Ciara, you know? That way if something happens, there's at least one person in each boat who knows what they're doing."

"That's a great idea!" Ciara jumped in enthusiastically. "And then we can teach you guys so you know for next time."

"All I know is, if I'm going in one of those crazy little boats, it *better* be with someone who knows what she's doing," AJ said. "I mean, the party boat was one thing, but . . . look how close those things are to the water."

"Well, you should definitely stick with me, then," Ciara said, wondering why AJ was acting so weird. He couldn't actually be scared, could he? "I've been kayaking since I was a kid."

"What do you think?" Kevin asked Heidi. "You want to let me take you for a spin?"

Ciara applauded inwardly. In his new sunglasses, black tank top, and flip-flops, he looked like the picture of confidence—the little pep talk she'd given him while they waited for AJ and Heidi to show up must have worked. If there was one thing Ciara knew from her past, it was how to boost a guy's ego: she'd complimented Kevin on the way his arms looked with their new summer tan and laughed even harder than usual at all his jokes. Plus, she hadn't mentioned Star Wars since they left the diner.

"Sure," Heidi said brightly. Ciara felt bad for a moment—she could tell that under her sunny exterior, Heidi was struggling to hide her disappointment at not getting to go with AJ. But she quickly regained her composure and chirped, "Sounds good to me!" Good ol' Heidi. Always enthusiastic. Ciara hoped she'd be feeling more enthusiastic about Kevin by the time their little expedition was done. It would be up to Kevin to turn up the charm like she knew he could.

Ciara instructed AJ to get in the front of the kayak—being in the back would give her the power to steer, which made sense since she'd done this before. "Hey, Kev-lar," AJ called as Ciara slowly paddled their boat away from the dock. "If I die out there, make sure you cash in on my death by producing a lot of posthumous albums like Biggie and Tupac, okay?"

"No prob, bro." Kevin laughed. "But I think you'll be all right. That big orange life vest on your shoulders isn't for looks, you know."

Heidi was giggling from the front of the blue kayak she was sharing with Kevin, and Ciara took that as a good sign. She threw Kevin a covert wink as they glided away from the dock side by side, their paddles making comforting splashing sounds as they dipped into the water and rose dripping from its sparkling surface. The ocean that afternoon was a brilliant blue, and the sun was warm on her back. Seagulls circled high above them, keening into the clean ocean air, and the repetitive rowing motion propelling the boat forward made Ciara feel strong and sure. But the most magnificent thing about the day was the gleaming muscles of AJ's biceps and shoulders peeking out from under his life vest. They were so beautiful that she completely forgot all the witty conversation she'd rehearsed in her head.

"Hey, I think I see some sea otters out that way," Kevin said, turning his boat to the left.

"Oh, really?" Heidi sounded excited. "I'd love to see some up close. Like, not in an aquarium or whatever."

"Let's go. See you guys!" Kevin called over his shoulder, paddling away from them.

"I think there's a cool little cove over this way," Ciara told AJ, heading in the opposite direction. "It's got a sand strip where we can get out and tan for a while if you're into that."

"As long as you keep this thing upright until we get there," AJ joked.

"I told you, I know what I'm doing," Ciara said, her confidence returning. She let silence settle over the boat for three long strokes of the paddle, savoring their quiet, perfect moment alone together. "So did you have fun on the party boat last night?" she asked after a while.

"Yeah," AJ said, not turning to look at her. "Kevin's getting really good on the decks."

"You looked like you were having a good time dancing with Heidi," Ciara probed.

"She got kinda wild, yeah," AJ said.

"How are things going with her?" Ciara asked, going for broke. She didn't get a lot of time alone with AJ, and now was her chance to find out how he really felt.

"Whatever." AJ shook his head. His voice sounded cold and distant. "I'm really not all about that right now. The last time I was really into someone, it didn't work out, so I'm just focusing on my music for now."

Ciara fought to contain her happiness. Every time Heidi talked about AJ, it sounded like he couldn't get enough of her, but now he was acting like he barely knew she existed. Ciara's chances were totally better than she'd imagined.

"What if you met someone who cared about the music as much as you do?" she asked quietly.

AJ finally turned to look at her, his head cocked in a half grin. Her heart nearly did a swan dive out of her chest and into the water. "Thanks, but I don't really like Kevin like that," he said.

Ciara laughed. She was glad that her heart had decided to stay put. She decided it was time to change the subject. "Speaking of your career, how are the new songs coming for the Coup show?" she asked.

AJ had already returned his attention to the water ahead, but she could see him warming to the topic just from the way his head sat a little higher on his shoulders. "Pretty good," he said. "I'm trying for real simple, strong stuff—the kind of songs you can't get out of your head, like D4L and Nelly. Just drumbeats, maybe a synth line, and a really catchy hook. I'd love to get some backup singers."

"That would be great," Ciara said. "I was reading on Billboard's website that visual appeal is half of what makes or breaks a band, and having girls onstage would really add complexity to the picture you create as a group."

"I never thought of that," AJ said admiringly. Then, even more admiringly: "Hey, you sit around reading the Billboard website?"

"I think the music business is fascinating," Ciara said. "I want to be an entertainment lawyer, remember?"

"Oh, right," AJ said. "Damn, that's so cool."

"Actually," Ciara continued, "I have some plans for

the B-Dizzy Crew. I've been researching underground hip-hop websites, and if you guys mix a demo, we can pretend to leak it as an official sneak preview. That's how a lot of major unrepresented groups are getting their start now. If you create Internet buzz, you eventually catch the attention of the A and R people from the major labels who are trolling those sites looking for the next big thing."

"Wow." AJ had swiveled 180 degrees in his seat to look at her, a big, crooked smile on his face. Ciara's heart stood up and took a bow. "You're a genius, you know that? You and me together, we could make a great team."

It was hard to tell if he was talking about a business team or a romantic one, but a girl could always hope. Ciara was so busy staring into his gorgeous almond-shaped eyes that she didn't even notice the large wave rolling toward their kayak. Turning back to resume paddling, AJ caught the swell approaching their side and cried, "Oh, crap!"

The wave crashed over their heads even as Ciara dug her paddle frantically into the water, trying unsuccessfully to keep the boat upright.

And then she was surrounded by water, the ocean rushing in her ears, her eyes closing themselves instinctively against the salt. Abruptly, she felt her head breaking the surface, her body buoyed up by the life vest. Shaking the water from her hair and opening her eyes, she looked around wildly, blinking against the suddenly too-bright sunlight.

She realized with relief that she was still clutching her paddle tightly in both hands—getting back to shore would be almost impossible without it. The boat was a few feet away, floating upside down, but she couldn't find AJ. Ciara thrashed her arms frantically, propelling herself in a circle and looking all around. Her heart jackhammered in her chest.

"AJ!" she called, her voice sounding wild and lost.

"What the . . ." His voice came from the other side of the capsized kayak. She swam quickly around it, and relief washed through her when she saw his head bobbing up and down on the water.

His eyes narrowed as she approached. "I thought you said you knew how to drive this thing!"

Ciara suddenly wished she had just gone ahead and drowned. No matter what she did to win AJ, nothing worked. It seemed like the more she tried, the more she ended up looking like a jerk.

"Look, I didn't see the wave, okay?" she said. "Now you can either keep chewing me out, or you can help me get this thing upright again."

She looked past AJ and noticed his paddle floating several yards away, the motion of the tide gently drawing it out to sea.

"Quick, get your paddle!" she said. "We don't want it to float away."

"You want me to swim all the way over there?" AJ squawked, his voice rising in panic.

Her exasperation swelled higher than the wave that had knocked them over. "The sooner you get your paddle, the sooner we can get upright and moving again," she explained.

"I'm not sure I want to go any farther out than this," AJ said. His eyes jerked sharply from side to side, his jaw twitching.

"Fine," Ciara said. AJ was obviously panicking, and since she hadn't already died of embarrassment, she figured she might as well try and get them out of there. She thrust her paddle toward AJ. "Hold on to this," she said, already swimming away. She could almost feel AJ's eyes boring into her back.

"Okay," she said, returning a moment later with his paddle in her hand. "All we have to do is flip the boat over and get into it, and we'll be fine."

"What if we can't?" AJ asked. His voice was very small.

"Of course we can," Ciara snapped. Why did AJ have to choose this moment, of all times, to channel his inner whiny toddler? "And even if we can't, see the shoreline? It's less than half a mile away. We can swim if we have to."

"You never told me you have to be on the Olympic breaststroke team to go in one of these things," AJ muttered.

Ciara held out the paddles. "Hold these," she commanded, shoving them at him before approaching the boat's side. The first time her dad had taken her out kayaking, they'd gone through a short safety course on how to right the boat if it flipped. But that was years ago. If only she could remember what they'd said . . .

Ciara contemplated the boat from all angles. Approaching the side, she got one shoulder under it and gave it a good shove. To her surprise, the boat rocked easily back into an upright position.

"Step one," she said pointedly to AJ. He wouldn't meet her gaze.

Getting into the boat was more difficult. First, she grasped its side and attempted to haul herself over the edge, the way you'd pull yourself up out of a swimming pool. The boat rocked back and forth slightly before flipping over on top of her, and she found herself having to wedge her shoulder back under the edge to right it. Swimming around the front, she tried bracing herself on the bow so that her weight was evenly balanced across both sides. She had almost managed to climb in when she lost her grip on the slippery Plexiglas front and went flying back into the water.

"I'm gonna need your help," she cried to AJ, who was morosely treading water a few feet away. "Can you hold one side while I climb in the other?"

"Whatever," AJ grumbled. But he did what she asked, swimming toward her with the paddles trailing awkwardly behind.

With AJ steadying the side of the boat, Ciara was able to climb in pretty easily. Once she was resettled, she leaned way to the side and placed the ends of both paddles in the water, redistributing the weight so AJ could climb in.

"Man," he said, flopping into his seat and resting his forehead on the bow for a moment in mock prayer. "I thought we were going to die out there." There was no joking tone to his voice now. His relief was palpable. He had really, truly been scared—and worse, he knew she knew it.

The paddle felt twice as heavy in Ciara's hands as she steered the boat back to the dock. With each dip of the blades into the water, her mood sank lower and lower. Instead of ratcheting up the flirt factor with AJ, she'd scared him half to death and nearly drowned him. Worse, she'd taken charge of the situation and made him feel incompetent and unmanly. Guys liked for girls to pretend to rely on them in desperate situations, and she'd gone barreling ahead and righted the boat while he was still flashing back to the first time he saw *Jaws*.

She recalled the fantasy she'd had earlier that day of her and AJ chilling on the small sandbar in the deserted, romantic cove, their hands inching gingerly closer and closer until their fingers were intertwined, whispering secrets as the sun made its long, lazy journey westward through the sky. The vision popped as she felt her soaked hair clinging to the back of her neck, and the brisk sea breeze against her damp skin felt cold and unwelcoming.

"Hey, stop frowning!" AJ said from the boat's bow. He had turned and was looking at her from under his long, perfect black lashes. "You look cute when you're wet."

What the hell was *that* supposed to mean? Did he really think she looked cute, or was he just messing with her head? She wondered how she could possibly look cute with her wild curls straggling down her back in limp, oily strands. Obviously, AJ was joking around at her expense—just like he'd been doing ever since he'd laid eyes on the kayak.

AJ forced his face into a grin. "Look, sorry if I was a little harsh out there," he said quietly.

"It's cool," Ciara said flippantly. She tried to smile, but it was a pretty shoddy effort. It was clear that AJ could see how unhappy she was and was just trying to cheer her up. She knew he didn't mean a word of it. He thought she was reckless and pushy—hardly even make-out material, let alone a potential girlfriend. And then there was the way he'd acted like a petulant kid when things didn't go exactly right. Didn't he realize that behavior like that messed with her vision of him as the perfect boy? Guys as hot and confident as AJ weren't supposed to freak out like that. They were supposed to be cool and collected in the face of an emergency. If this were a music video, he would have scooped her up in his arms and planted a firm, comforting kiss on her lips instead of nearly peeing in his swim trunks while she did all the work. It wasn't a side of AJ she liked, and she hoped she wouldn't see it again.

Heidi and Kevin were already waiting for them when they pulled into the dock. "You guys go for a dip?" Kevin asked. "You're all wet."

"I know," Ciara said dully. Kevin was smiling, which must mean that things had gone well out there with Heidi.

"We totally crashed into a ten-foot wave!" AJ said. "But we handled it all right."

Sure . . . like he had handled anything. She had done it all.

"Wow, you're so brave," Heidi cooed, batting her eyes at him. "We saw sea otters. They were sooo cute!" She turned her sparkling eyes on Kevin. "Do your sea otter impression for them. You guys have to check this out—Kevin was cracking me up the whole way back."

"I gotta hit the girls' room," Ciara said, feeling majorly uninterested in Kevin's otter impression. A small shard of jealousy lodged in her chest. Obviously, Kevin's afternoon had gone a lot better than hers. She turned and headed for the restrooms.

"Oh, man, me too!" Heidi hurried after her. She caught up with her just as Ciara slipped into one of the stalls. "Kayaking was such a great idea," she said from behind the metal barrier. "How much fun was that?"

"It was all right," Ciara said, trying not to blow a gasket. She knew she would have felt happier for Kevin's success if she weren't so annoyed at her own disastrous afternoon.

"Kevin just kept cracking me up the whole time," Heidi continued. "He's so funny. Hey, what's up with you and him, anyway? You two have been spending a ton of time together."

"We're just friends," Ciara said through gritted teeth. She was glad to be safe in the stall so Heidi couldn't see her glaring.

"Are you sure?" Heidi persisted. "Because I could totally see you guys together. You'd actually make a great couple. And then you and Kevin and me and AJ could double date!"

Ciara could have cried. If Heidi thought she and Kevin were getting something going, Operation Woo-ha was even more of a disaster than she had thought.

Chapter Twelve

You can find it on the rack in your record store
If you get the record, then your thoughts are adored
—A Tribe Called Quest

S o how are things going with AJ?" Ciara asked. She
and Heidi were taking a break between the breakfast
and lunch rushes at the café, sitting at a table on the
deck overlooking the ocean and sharing a spinach and
sun-dried tomato omelet.

It was an overcast morning a few days after the kayaking fiasco. Only a few blankets were sprinkled across the
clean stretch of sand between the café and the surf line.
Unless the weather cleared up, it would probably be a
slow day at work.

"Oh, they're usually pretty good," Heidi said.

"Usually?" Ciara probed.

"Well, most of the time, he's really sweet," Heidi said. "But then he'll, like, go off into his own world, and when I ask what's up, he just says he's thinking about the crew or whatever."

"AJ always says that," Ciara said. "He's starting to sound like a scratched CD."

"Yeah, and sometimes I think it's not just his music," Heidi confessed, looking out over the ocean. "Like, sometimes he really wants to make out, but then all of a sudden he'll stop and get really distant and say he needs time alone. It's kind of frustrating. I mean, it's not like I need him to vow eternal devotion or anything, but if it's just because I'm inexperienced and doing a bad job or whatever, I wish he'd just tell me. I'd rather know I'm doing something wrong than keep making a fool of myself."

"I'm sure you're not doing anything wrong," Ciara assured her. She felt bad for Heidi, who still seemed so insecure sometimes under her snug-fitting tank tops and platinum bob. "But maybe you just need someone a little more open. AJ can be really complex—I'm sure it gets frustrating."

Ciara knew it was frustrating for *her*. She was still trying to figure out what the deal was with the whole kayaking debacle. Obviously, AJ knew he'd acted like a spaz. The one time she'd seen him since then, he'd barely said two words to her and hadn't been able to meet her eyes. She wished there was some way she could tell him she'd forgiven him. Everyone had flaws, even a guy as amazing as AJ. He was probably just stressed about the Coup show, which would be a huge deal for anyone, let alone a perfectionist like him. Maybe once they were together, she could help him get over his obvious fear of water. The old Ciara might have gotten sick of AJ after one little setback, but the new one would stand by her man for the long haul.

"But AJ's so hot!" Heidi protested. "Where else am I going to find a guy who looks like that? I keep hoping we'll bump into Jude so he can see how much better I'm doing now."

Ciara bit down hard into a chewy sun-dried tomato. Was that all AJ was to Heidi—a cheap way to get back at her ex? She thought bitterly that she could probably replace AJ with a cardboard cutout of Usher and Heidi wouldn't even notice.

"There are plenty of guys around as good-looking as AJ," Ciara fibbed. "And a lot of them are more open and funny and less moody. Don't you think you'd be happier with someone like that?"

"Maybe," Heidi said slowly. "But I haven't really met anyone who fits the bill."

"Are you sure?" Ciara asked, attempting to mentally beam a picture of Kevin into Heidi's head. She envisioned Kevin on the beach, taking off his sunglasses and smiling as the wind tousled his hair. How could Heidi not go for a guy like that?

"Well, actually," Heidi said conspiratorially, "remember that guy from Smoothie City? He sent me a really cute e-mail the other day."

Ciara pictured Kevin's face melting into a frown.

"That burnout with the stupid tattoo?" she asked.

"He's not a burnout!" Heidi protested. "He goes to college. And I thought the tattoo was kind of cute. But I told him I was seeing someone else."

"You mean AJ?" Ciara asked carefully.

"I don't even know if that's true, though." Heidi sighed. "I mean, we're totally not official or anything like I was with Jude. Or like he was with Marlene."

"Who still doesn't know about any of this, right?" Ciara clarified.

"Oh gosh, no," Heidi said. "And it's so weird because, like, she used to be one of my best friends, but now that I'm messing around with AJ, I can't talk to her about anything anymore. I feel like if she just looks at me hard enough, she'll know what's been going on."

"Are you sure she'd care?" Ciara asked. "I mean, she dumped him, right?"

"Yeah, but still . . ." Heidi fidgeted in her seat. "I mean, any way you cut it, it's kind of crappy to sneak around with your good friend's ex just a couple of months after they broke up. Like, I didn't even call her about the boat party. I told myself she was probably working early the next day, but . . . well, I wasn't sure. And then sometimes I wonder if she's really as over him as she says. She gets pretty cranky every time the subject of groupies comes up."

Ciara thought of Em back in LA. She'd always pretended to Em that she was happy Em had finally found love with Tim, but Ciara was starting to realize how much she'd resented that rift in their friendship from the get-go. Em had still tried to stay friends, but it was Ciara who couldn't take feeling like a third wheel and kept pushing her away. Of course, it hadn't helped when Em had started harping on her to change her love life, either.

"That's why I'm so glad I have you," Heidi continued, giving Ciara a wide, genuine smile. "Things are weird between me and Marlene right now, but I can talk to you about anything."

"I'm glad you can trust me," Ciara said. The irony was so strong it made her teeth hurt. She felt like the biggest snake in the world.

*   *   *

"Hey, you," Kevin greeted her as she ducked into the passenger seat of his blue Acura.

"Whatup, Kev?" Ciara clicked her seat belt into place. "Want to give me the post-kayaking report?"

As he pulled out of the beach club's parking lot, Kevin filled her in on his conversation with Heidi in the boat (mostly small talk) and how much she had loved the sea otters. "It was almost like being with the old Heidi again," Kevin said. "It was nice to see her excited over animals again instead of putting on too much makeup and talking about shaking her tail feather. But in terms of romantic vibes? I don't really know. She laughed at a lot of my jokes, so maybe that's a good sign. But she wasn't exactly begging to be Mrs. Kev-lar by the end of the ride, either." Instead of pouting, Kevin seemed to be in a pretty good mood. Maybe it was because, no matter what had happened, it couldn't have been as bad as Ciara's kayaking debacle with AJ. "So how'd it go for you?" Kevin asked, as if he could read her thoughts.

"You mean besides almost drowning him?"

Kevin laughed. "He told me later he was scared to death. But I think he's recovered."

"I wish I'd known about his deep-water phobia." Ciara sighed. "That really didn't go as planned."

"He'll get over it," Kevin assured her. "I think in his own way, he's starting to see how amazing you really are."

"Really?" Ciara asked. She could feel herself flushing slightly. "What makes you say that?"

"Oh, nothing concrete." Kevin was suddenly concentrating very intensely on the road. "It's just that you keep doing all these cool things like . . . well, like teaching us all how to kayak in the first place. I mean, he's got to see how great you are eventually. He'd be dumb not to."

"Thanks!" Ciara's blush grew hotter. It was weird to have Kevin compliment her like that but also kind of nice. It made her feel secure in a way she never quite did around AJ. With him, she was always walking on eggshells, terrified she was going to screw everything up.

Kevin pulled into a nondescript shopping plaza and stopped the car. "You up for digging through some record crates?"

"You know me," Ciara said. "I'm up for anything."

Kevin led her to a storefront with a large blue sign over it that said Satellite West in bright, spray-painted letters. As he pushed open the door, a funky speed garage track came bouncing out at them. The walls of the store were covered in rainbow-colored graffiti, everything from small black-and-white tags to large, elaborately shaded pictures, and a row of smoked-glass listening booths stood against one wall. It was totally different than the big, generic music stores she was used to visiting in LA.

Kevin went straight to the Soul section and began rif-fling through the records. Ciara stood next to him, sud-denly über-conscious of the fact that the dreadlocked girl at the cash register was giving her outfit (the simple black shorts and white T-shirt she always wore to work) the once-over. She felt decidedly unhip.

"AJ wants our sound to have more female vocals," Kevin explained, picking out records and making a small pile on top of the next bin. "So I'm looking for stuff to sample."

"Oh." To keep from looking like she didn't belong there, Ciara began flipping through the bin in front of her. Black women in sparkly lipstick and evening gowns smiled at her from most of the covers. There were few names she'd actually heard of. It was depressing to think of how many people just never made it in the music business, even if they got as far as producing an album.

"So I'm thinking of throwing a beach party," Kevin said suddenly. "We did it last year, and it was off the hook. You know, sneak in a keg, set up some turntables, make a bonfire, camp out. You can usually get permis-sion from the beach club to do stuff like that as long as you promise to keep the noise level down and take responsibility for anyone swimming without a lifeguard."

"Sounds like fun," Ciara said.

Kevin gave her a cute, crooked smile. "Glad you

think so," he said. "Oh, and it could be a chance to get some Woo-haing in too. I forgot to tell you that AJ said the other day that Heidi's taste in music is really starting to get on his nerves."

"Really? He actually said that?"

"Well . . . he said that if he had to listen to one more Pussycat Dolls tune, he was going to spew," Kevin said. "I just assumed he was talking about Heidi. You know, she's all into them and stuff."

"Maybe . . . ," Ciara said. But she still felt skeptical. Sure, she wanted AJ more than ever, but she was getting tired of chasing and chasing without ever reaching her goal. It was starting to hurt her ego, and she missed her old confidence.

"Come on," Kevin urged. He placed a friendly hand on Ciara's shoulder. "I've seen the way he looks at you. He totally thinks you're hot—plus you guys have the making-it-big thing in common." He shook his head like he couldn't quite understand what motivated that kind of drive, but he was smiling.

"You think?" Ciara asked. Kevin's flattery was working. She already felt a little better. Maybe she could give it one more go.

"I *know*," Kevin assured her. "Anyway, it'll be sweet: a nice moonlit night, some great tunes and beer. Anything could happen."

"Maybe," Ciara said, melting a little more.

"Well, the Ciara I know doesn't turn down a good party." Kevin picked up the stack of records he'd made and motioned for her to follow him to a listening booth. There was just enough room in it for him to stand at the turntable while she sat on the tiny velvet-cushioned bench. He put a record on and a shrill, screeching voice filled the booth.

"Um, *no.*" Kevin quickly replaced the record in its sleeve. The next one featured a low, sultry female vocalist with a cool piano line that immediately had him bobbing his head.

"Oh, I just remembered," Ciara said suddenly. "My mom's in town this weekend. I'll have to make sure seeing her doesn't interfere with the beach party." Her face twitched into a frown in spite of herself. All summer long, she'd thought that when she finally saw her mom, she'd be able to triumphantly tell her she wasn't returning to LA. But now she didn't feel so triumphant. So far, things hadn't worked out quite the way she'd planned. Without the perfect boy, was there any point in sticking around? If she got frustrated and returned to her old ways, why even bother staying in Santa Barbara? Then she'd have a bad rep in two schools instead of just one.

"You don't seem too psyched about it," Kevin observed.

"I could more or less live without my mom for the time being," Ciara said. "It's been nice not having to deal with her so much this summer. In fact, I was kind of considering staying in Santa Barbara this fall. Not just to get away from her but just . . . well . . ." She trailed off, realizing she'd just given Kevin way too much info. Her plans to stay in Santa Barbara were top secret. Why was she suddenly giving everything away?

"It would be great if you stayed here," Kevin said encouragingly.

"Yeah, but it's just confusing," Ciara said. "I thought I'd come here and everything would be great just because I was out of LA and away from my mom, but now I'm not so sure. Heck, I don't even know why I'm telling you all this. I'm going to shut up now."

But Kevin just stood there and listened, his eyes fixed intently on her. "Not to get all Dr. Phil on you or anything," he said. "But it sounds like you're trying to escape more than just your mom."

Ciara felt her face grow hot. Why was she even having this conversation with Kevin—and in the middle of a record store?

Kevin shrugged. "Hey, it's cool if you don't want to talk about it. When my parents split back in middle school, there were like three weeks where I didn't go anywhere or talk to anyone. All I did was sit in my room listening to records. That's when I really got into spinning and scratching."

He turned and lifted the needle abruptly, putting the record back in its sleeve and replacing it with another soulful female vocal track.

"The divorce has nothing to do with it," Ciara snapped. "Actually, I'm happy about it."

"No offense," Kevin said. "But you don't really look happy."

"I *am*!" Ciara insisted. "All my parents did when they were together was fight, but they were hardly ever together because my mom was off running around."

Her hands flew to her mouth as soon as the words were out. She had just given away *way* too much. What was it about being with Kevin in the listening booth that made her flap her trap? It was almost like a confessional. But Kevin was hardly a priest.

"Look, all I'm saying is, whether it's the right thing for your parents or not, it can still hurt you. I know it hurt me."

Ciara couldn't even look at him. She drew her knees up close to her chest and rested her chin on them, letting the singer's voice soar around her head. She tried to push Kevin's words out of her mind, but they stayed in there, ricocheting off the sides of her brain like the singer's voice against the walls of the tiny booth.

He was wrong, of course. She wasn't hurt by the divorce—she was happy her parents were both doing what they wanted to do. Sure, she resented her mom for cheating. Who wouldn't? She'd gotten mad when Jude Law cheated on Sienna Miller too. But it wasn't like she took it personally.

At the moment, though, it wasn't even worth thinking about. Kevin was dividing the records into stacks to buy and stacks to put back. His blunt-cut hair fell haphazardly over his forehead and into his eyes. Ciara spontaneously stood up and used the palm of her hand to push the thatch of hair away from Kevin's face.

Kevin looked up, surprised. "What are you doing?" he asked.

"Trying to see what you'd look like with a different haircut," she explained. "You've had the same hair forever. It might be time to go for something new."

"Something new for *the ladies*?" Kevin asked in his funny-man voice, wiggling his eyebrows.

"For a certain lady named Heidi, definitely," Ciara said.

"You know, ordinarily I'd ask if you really thought she'd go for it," Kevin said. "But she really liked my new shades and that T-shirt you helped me pick out the other day, so I think I'm just going to defer to your superior judgment on this one."

"Are you saying you'll let me drag you to my favorite salon here?" Ciara asked.

"Sure." Kevin sighed. "As long as they don't try to wax my eyebrows or anything."

"I'll do what I can to preserve your delicate masculinity." Ciara laughed as they exited the store. Joking around with Kevin had lifted a lot of the family-induced funk she'd dropped into just moments before. She was already starting to feel better.

Chapter Thirteen

The summer days are gone too soon
You shoot the moon
And miss completely
And now you're left to face the gloom
                                        —*Norah Jones*

This is going to be the best night ever!" Heidi said, heaving a tent from the trunk of her car and dropping it with a heavy thud on the pavement of the beach club parking lot.

"I'm looking forward to it," Ciara said. She meant it, too. Not long after the kayaking disaster, AJ had started e-mailing and texting her with questions about marketing strategies for the B-Dizzy Crew, and in the last couple of days, things had even gotten a little flirtatious. Like when AJ wrote that he'd think of his new songs as a success if they got hotties like her dancing onstage (followed by an emoticon wink) or saying that their new song was partly inspired by her.

Ciara felt like she was holding the night ahead of them in the palm of her hand. It was a beautiful, clear, moonlit evening with stars gleaming like tiny ice chips in the sky, and the salty ocean air had a wild, intoxicating smell that made her feel like anything could happen. Lust and romance seemed to sweep in with every wave that caressed the shore. Tomorrow she might have to face her mom, but tonight she was going to make it happen. Tonight was hers.

"I can smell the bonfire from here," Heidi said, and sure enough, the tangy scent of wood smoke drifted toward them on a gentle breeze. Farther down the beach, in a secluded area separated from the road by a tall dune, they could see the blaze of the fire and hear the seductive bass of a bumping sound system. As they approached, they saw bodies clustered around the fire and the keg, sipping beer from plastic cups and laughing in the moonlight. Several tents already dotted the party site, and a shade structure had been set up to protect the generator, turntables, and speakers, which blasted an upbeat house track.

They found a place to set up their tent, then wandered over to the fire, greeting friends of Heidi's from school and people Ciara had met at D-John's parties along the way. An enthusiastic terrier rushed toward them, wagging its tail as if trying to shake it off its butt.

"Aw, isn't it the cutest?" Heidi cooed, squatting down to pet the dog. "I wonder whose it is?"

"I'm borrowing him for the evening." Kevin emerged from the shade structure and clapped. Ciara smiled to herself at her handiwork—the new haircut framed his face beautifully, showing off his strong, square jaw and smiling eyes. The dog immediately hurried back to him and sat at his feet, staring up expectantly and still wagging his tail like he was trying to sweep the sand off the beach. "He's my neighbor's, but when I said I was doing a beach campout, he begged me to take him. Apparently, Woofie is a big fan of the beach."

"Aw, Woofie!" Heidi looked down at the dog with stars in her eyes. "You're so cute! I wish you were my little puppy."

Ciara couldn't help admiring Kevin's strategy. He'd told her in a text message that he had a surprise secret weapon that any girl would go crazy over, but this was better than anything she could have predicted. Heidi's inner animal freak was coming out all over the place.

"I have to walk him," Kevin said to them. "You girls want to come?"

"Heck, yeah!" Heidi said.

"I'm going to stay here and warm up by the fire," Ciara said, wondering why he was inviting her too. Didn't he want the time alone with Heidi?

She waved to the two of them as they disappeared down the beach, two tall shadows with a tiny one dancing and nipping at their heels.

"Hey, girl!" a voice said close to her ear. She turned to see Marlene, wearing a comfy white velour tracksuit and holding a beer.

Ciara greeted her with a hug. "Good to see you," she said genuinely. "You haven't been around much."

"I've been working a lot," Marlene said. "And kind of doing my own thing. I started taking yoga—it's great. You should come sometime."

"I'd like that," Ciara said. "Have you been here for long?"

"Yeah, I was over by the fire trying to talk to AJ for a while, but he's acting all weird again." Marlene made a face. "Probably wondering if this gig's going to launch him to superstardom or whatever."

"I know," Ciara agreed, even though it was actually what she liked best about AJ. "But if that's what he wants . . ."

"Exactly." A sharp buzzing came from Marlene's pocket, and she fished out her phone. "Crap, that's probably my cousin. I said I'd meet her at the parking lot and help her carry her stuff back here. Catch you later, okay?"

Ciara turned and headed toward the fire, guiltily relieved that Marlene had to disappear for a bit. Her heart skipped in her chest when she saw AJ sitting by the fireside, staring intently at the flames. People talked and laughed around him, but he didn't appear to be part of the group. She wondered what he was thinking about. New song lyrics? The next step to stardom? *Her?* She was about to join him when she had a thought. Stopping by the keg, she poured two plastic cups of beer and walked toward AJ, balancing them carefully in each hand so they wouldn't spill down the front of her green crocheted Miss Sixty tank top. It wasn't that she was trying to get them drunk. If AJ had to be drunk to want her, she would rather not have him. Then again, if it helped him forget about whatever was bothering him . . . well, that was kind of a plus too, wasn't it?

"I brought you something," she said quietly, coming up behind him. AJ jerked around, startled—he'd clearly been deep in thought about *something*. But his face relaxed into a smile when he saw her, and he patted the patch of sand next to him. Ciara handed him the plastic cup of beer and sat down, her thigh rubbing against his as she did. It was just for a brief moment, but the spot where they'd touched seemed to warm faster in the heat from the fire.

"Thanks." AJ held up his glass for a toast.

"Here's to a great night," she said, tapping the rim of her cup against his.

"And great company," AJ replied, his eyes holding hers like magnets. Just looking at him made her feel more alive than she had all day—maybe even all summer. Sitting next to AJ, with their eyes locked like that, made the air seem fresher, the fire hotter, the beer more tart and sweet and intoxicating.

"You think?" Ciara asked. Their shoulders brushed briefly, and her skin tingled like there wasn't enough of it to cover her body.

"Well, yeah, Ciara," AJ said, turning to her, his eyes so dark and deep she could have fallen into them and swum around for a while. "I mean, you've done so much for the B-Dizzy Crew—all your help with marketing and your great ideas and just your constant support. I'm not sure I ever really thanked you enough for that."

"You're welcome," she breathed. The way AJ was thanking her, it almost sounded like he was practicing to accept a Grammy—but the way he was looking into her eyes was much more intimate. Her whole body was full of wanting him: all the longing that had built up over the summer, all the nights she had dreamed of holding him and woken up with her arms grasping at empty air, all the plotting she had done with Kevin to get him swarmed around inside her, desperate to get out. If something real—and passionate—and very, very sexy didn't happen soon, she was going to explode.

"I mean, you're amazing too," she continued. "You're so smart and talented and . . . I just know there's so much more to you than anyone knows about. And I want to get to know you more. I want to take this deeper."

She couldn't hold back anymore. This was *it*—the moonlight, the music, and AJ all converged in the palm of her hand. The night was hers. She leaned forward, closed her eyes, and pressed her lips to his.

Ciara couldn't believe she was finally kissing AJ! Just the realization that she'd gotten exactly what she wanted turned her skeleton into a warm, soupy liquid. It short-circuited her brain, made her feel like she was jumping off a cliff and into the new, perfect life she'd craved for so long.

The knowledge sent an exhilarating calm buzzing through her. When they finally pulled apart, Ciara could almost see cartoon hearts popping out of their heads. She couldn't stop the dopey smile from spreading across her face.

"That was amazing," she said in a voice that barely sounded like her own. It was dizzy and breathy, like . . . well, like Heidi's voice when she had told her about their first kiss on top of the roller coaster.

Ciara had to force the image of Heidi out of her head. It was ruining the moment—*her* moment. She wasn't ready to chase the sweet taste of victory out of her mouth with a sour dose of guilt.

"Yeah," AJ said slowly. But his face registered something other than post-kiss bliss. "Yeah," he said again, more softly, as he moved away from her on the sand, hugging his knees and looking down to avoid her eyes.

"Are you okay?" Ciara put a hand on his back. Maybe he was just trying to figure out a way of saying he wanted to take this to the next level. Or maybe he was wondering what to do about Heidi, how to let her down nicely. Either way, Ciara was sure he that felt the same way she did: that they were kindred souls meant to be together, their fate sealed by that kiss.

"I don't know how to say this," he began.

"Take your time," Ciara said, dipping her head to try and look him in the eye.

AJ took a deep breath. "I'm kind of confused," he said. "Ever since I broke up with Marlene, all these girls have been after me, and I don't always know what to do about it. Heidi's all over me, but sometimes I feel like she's just using me to get back at Jude. And you were cold at the beginning of the summer, but you've been really flirty ever since. Plus, all these girls keep giving me their numbers after shows, like I'm actually going to call up people I don't even know. Part of me likes the attention, but part of me knows that it's not really about me—it's about something they see in me that isn't really there."

The cartoon hearts floating above Ciara's head began to deflate. Was AJ trying to say that she was just another girl who was into him? Didn't he see that they had so much more than that?

"I thought it was different with us," she whispered.

AJ finally met her eyes, giving her a rueful smile. "In some ways, it is," he said. "You're great, and you obviously really care about what happens to my career. That means a lot to me. But I'm still kind of getting over Marlene, and having all these girls chase me is a real mind freak. Before Marlene, I was Star Wars boy. I was playing with a toy lightsaber. Girls weren't exactly banging my door down. I'm not used to this."

"So what are you saying?" Ciara asked. She felt like she'd just swallowed fiberglass.

AJ sighed. "I guess just that I need time to think," he said quietly, putting a hand on her knee. An infuriatingly fraternal hand.

Hurt boiled in Ciara's throat. She had to will herself

not to cry. "Well, maybe you should have thought of that before you kissed me," she said. She stood up quickly, and the beer rushed to her head. She swayed for a moment before catching her balance, realizing she was too close to the fire, too close to AJ and all the other people and the music and everything else. Then Ciara ran to her tent, kicking up sand behind her as she went. She could hear AJ calling her name, but she didn't turn around. Not this time. Maybe not ever again.

Chapter Fourteen

And on the topic of trust, it's just a matter of fact
That people bite back and fracture what's intact
—The Roots

Ciara sprinted until she got to the tent, suddenly glad that she and Heidi had set it up far enough away from the party that even the music was just a dull thump in the distance. Tears welled up in her eyes, and she let them fall freely down her cheeks as she tugged at the zipper, trying to get the door open so she could get inside and away from everything. She unrolled her sleeping bag and crawled inside, curling up in a ball with the synthetic fabric rubbing against her bare legs. Turning on her stomach, she buried her head in her arms and let the sobs overtake her. Everything had been so perfect, and with just a few words, AJ had shattered it.

She could still barely believe that he didn't see how incredibly right they were for each other. She was willing to support him in everything, be his main cheerleader and adviser in his budding music career. All she asked in return was for him to love her—or even to want her enough to not be able to resist her kisses. She was used to being the one who said no, who turned boys away when they wanted her the most. Now she was on the other end, and it didn't feel good at all.

The sleeping bag warmed around her, and her head grew heavy on her arms as her sobs slowly subsided. Maybe she would just take a little nap . . . and then she'd go back to the party with her head held high, as if nothing had ever happened, as if she hadn't just lost the one thing she'd been trying all summer to get. She could pick up the pieces from there. What else was there to do? All her plans were destroyed once and for all.

*   *   *

She didn't know if it was minutes or hours later when she heard a scuffling outside the tent, accompanied by a long, quavering wail. At first, she was scared—were there animals on the beach? And if so, why were they trying to get into her tent?

There was the long squeal of the zipper opening, and a platinum-blond head poked itself inside.

"Heidi," Ciara said, partly as a greeting and partly to assure herself that it really was her friend. Everything was dim in the moonlight.

"Yeah, hi." Heidi's voice was choked with tears. She sniffled loudly. "Sorry, did I wake you up?"

"No, that's cool," Ciara said groggily. Why was Heidi crying? Her blood suddenly chilled—had AJ told her about the kiss? What if Heidi was mad at her?

But Heidi didn't seem mad. Just very, very unhappy. She zipped the tent up behind her and collapsed on the air mattress next to Ciara, sniffling and whimpering.

"What's wrong?" Ciara asked.

"It's . . ." Heidi took a shaky breath and let out another volley of sobs. "AJ," she finished finally. "He said he's confused and needs time to think and doesn't want to hook up anymore."

Well, *that* line sure sounded familiar! Ciara wished she could tell Heidi she knew exactly how she felt, but of course that would give everything away. It was frustrating to be in such a similar situation and not be able to bond over it the way they could just talking about boys and friends in general back at the café.

"Everything was going so well," Heidi continued. "I mean, I had this great walk with Kevin and then I got back and I was ready to get seriously into making out with AJ when out of the blue he's all, 'We need to talk.' And that's when he dropped it on me."

Obviously, their kiss had triggered something in him. A tiny hope flitted through Ciara's head—maybe AJ had realized that they really *did* belong together, and he was trying to let Heidi down the easy way first. But then why hadn't he come and found her? She shooed the thought away. It wasn't doing any good, and she still had a crying friend on her hands. "I'm sorry," Ciara said quietly.

Heidi looked at her through her tears. "Well, it's not *your* fault," she said.

Guilt snaked its way through Ciara's gut. Little did Heidi realize that it actually was.

"I know, but I feel bad for you," Ciara said quickly. "I didn't think you'd be this upset. I thought AJ was just an outlet for Heidi the wild child."

"Well, maybe I was starting to want more than just hooking up. I don't know," Heidi said.

The guilt in Ciara's stomach seeped through her entire body. She felt awful. Would she still have gone for AJ if she'd known Heidi liked him as more than just a summer boy toy? It was a question she didn't want to even try to answer.

"Anyway, it's over now." Heidi let out a sigh that ended in a small sob. "I just . . . I kind of wish I'd never started anything with him in the first place. All I did was get myself hurt."

"What about Kevin?" Ciara asked, desperate for something—*anything*—to say to get Heidi to stop crying. The guilt was like a jackhammer drilling a hole in her brain.

"What *about* Kevin?" Heidi asked. "Why do you keep bringing him up?"

"You said you had a great walk with him," Ciara said. "Maybe he's really the right guy for you."

Heidi looked at Ciara like she'd just suggested a romance with an escaped convict. "Kevin's my friend," she said. "I could never think of him as anything more."

"Why?" Ciara asked. "He's really cute, and smart, and funny . . . plus he's an amazing DJ and he's always coming up with cool things to do."

"Yeah," Heidi said. "But he's just not for me."

Ouch. That would hurt Kevin once she told him about it. So much for Operation Woo-ha. Operation Loser was more like it. Why had they even bothered? People were so crazy when it came to who they chose to be with. Maybe the world would be a better place if everyone just stayed single and hung out with their friends.

"Okay." Ciara shrugged as if it had just been a

passing thought. "He's a nice guy, though," she couldn't help adding.

Heidi burst into a fresh cascade of sobs. "Listen, I have to get out of here," she said, swabbing at her leaking eyes with the back of her hand. "A party is the last place I want to be in a mood like this. I just want to go home, eat chocolate, and cry myself to sleep."

Ciara knew exactly what she meant. "I'll go with you," she offered.

"Really?" Heidi brightened. "Don't you want to stay and, like, scope hotties or dance or whatever?"

"Nah," Ciara said. She was already gathering up her sleeping bag. "I'd just as soon sleep in my own bed as on this leaky air mattress. Let's go."

"Cool."

At least it had made Heidi's tears stop. They climbed out of the tent and began taking it down.

"We should at least say good-bye to Kevin," Ciara said as they dragged the camping equipment across the beach. "And thank him for the party and stuff. I mean, he did plan most of it."

"Good idea," Heidi agreed. "I wouldn't mind giving Woofie a good-bye hug, either. He's such a cute dog."

They approached the campfire and scanned the faces around it, all glowing orange from the dancing flames.

None of them were Kevin's. He wasn't by the keg or even in the makeshift DJ booth.

D-John was spinning. "Haven't seen him in a while," he said when Ciara asked about Kevin. "Maybe he's down there."

He gestured down the beach toward the surf. A few couples had spread blankets out on the sand and were taking advantage of the darkness to make out. They looked like beached humpbacked whales silhouetted against the deep blue sky.

Heidi joined her. "I couldn't find him," she said. "Maybe he just went for a walk or something."

"Well, he's on at midnight," D-John said. "If he's not back here by then, I'll give you girls a call and you can join the search party."

"Thanks," Ciara said. She picked up her sleeping bag and followed Heidi across the beach to the parking lot.

All the power and energy she'd felt at the beginning of the night was gone. For a moment—just one—she had held the night in the palm of her hand. Now she was just a regular girl, holding nothing but a sleeping bag and leaving a party early because she didn't get the guy.

Chapter Fifteen

*Ain't a woman alive that could take my
mama's place*

—Tupac

thought about it and I'm sorry and I want you to stay in Santa Barbara so I can be with you forever," AJ said. They were alone on the party boat, sitting on a sleek leather couch just like the one in the living room of her old house in LA and looking out over the ocean. The boat had lost its railings, and as it pitched from side to side on the waves, the couch rolled back and forth on the deck. She realized lazily that she ought to be worried they would roll right off and into the ocean, but she was too busy staring deep into AJ's eyes, which seemed darker and more luminous than ever before.

"I want to be with you too." She sighed. She tilted her face up and sank into his kiss like a warm, luxurious bubble bath, letting it envelop her until their embrace was the only thing in the world.

The wind blew and the boat rocked and the couch slid back and forth, back and forth and she didn't care as their kiss went on and on and the couch slid toward the edge . . .

And suddenly the boat hit a wave and the couch went flying off the deck, the force jerking her and AJ apart and then she was falling toward the water, falling for an unnaturally long time past many stories of portholes, each of which had a curious face staring out of it at the boy and the girl and the couch all tumbling toward the ocean, which suddenly seemed very dark and scary and cold.

Someone screamed her name from the boat's deck, and she looked up to see Kevin quickly lowering a rope.

"Kevin!" she screamed, flailing her arms, trying to catch the rope. But it was too late. With a terrible splash, she hit the water and, in that moment, woke up to find herself wrapped in the sheet of her own bed, her heart thudding violently in her chest.

Had she yelled his name out loud? She listened for her father's footsteps—he'd come running in an instant if she screamed—but everything was quiet. Outside, the sky was the color of skim milk. The clock on her nightstand read 7:17.

She lay in bed for a long time, trying to fall back asleep and forget all about how she'd flubbed all her summer plans. But the events of the night before kept running through her head: the kiss with AJ and then his horrible speech about needing time to think, comforting Heidi in the tent after crying there herself, and then deciding to leave and trying to find Kevin and not being able to.

Kevin. Ciara wondered where he was. She lay in bed until she couldn't bear to be alone with herself anymore, then showered, dressed, and sat staring at the screen of her cell phone, wondering if it was too early to call.

She ended up sending him a text message, saying simply: *Tried to find you last night. R U ok?*

She was surprised when her phone buzzed just moments later. For some reason, hearing the familiar ring tone made her inordinately happy. Maybe she was just relieved to know that Kevin was all right.

I'm fine. Just got home.

It was all she needed to hear. Ciara was already gathering her car keys and heading out the door. As she drove to Kevin's house, she told herself that it would be easier for them to talk about Operation Woo-ha in person. Her phone buzzed again.

Where R U? Kevin had texted.

Coming over right now, she wrote back. She'd only been to Kevin's place once before, but the route felt familiar and comforting. She couldn't wait to see him and find out how his night had gone and where he'd disappeared to.

She pulled into his driveway and found Kevin in the kitchen, eating a bowl of Froot Loops. He'd just showered, but even with the scent of shampoo drifting from his freshly washed hair, he looked tired from the night before.

"I only got a couple hours of sleep," he explained. "Have you ever tried to sleep in a tent once the sun comes up? It's like a Dutch oven."

"I can imagine," Ciara said. Kevin finished his cereal and rinsed out the bowl before motioning for her to follow him to his studio. He flicked a switch at the top of the stairs to the basement, and a dim bulb lit their way down to the room he'd tricked out with a set of turntables, a kicking sound system, and egg crate foam on the walls to absorb sound. Crates of records were scattered around the room, and he'd tacked a poster of Qbert, his favorite DJ, to one of the walls. Ciara looked around in surprise. She'd never seen his studio and, aside from that time at Satellite West, had never seen so much vinyl in her life. So this was where Kevin spent hours by himself, putting together the sets she loved.

"Welcome to my world," Kevin joked when he noticed her gawking. He knelt in front of one of the crates and began digging through it, muttering something about having a track stuck in his head.

"So where'd you go last night?" Ciara asked, hovering awkwardly behind him. She told herself she would have found somewhere to sit, but every available surface was covered in records. "We looked everywhere for you."

"Oh." Kevin didn't turn around. "Marlene and I went for a walk."

She waited for him to elaborate, but he just kept flipping through the albums. Her stomach tightened as she pictured him strolling along the dark, empty beach with Marlene, their bare arms brushing. Had anything happened? Would he tell her if it had? She knew she could just come out and ask him, but the words stuck in her throat.

"What happened with AJ?" Kevin asked.

"I don't want to talk about it," Ciara said. She hesitated a moment before settling on the floor next to him, hugging her knees. The shampoo smell was even stronger up close.

Kevin looked over at her and raised an eyebrow, and that was all it took for her to spill the whole story of the night. When she got to the part about Heidi crying over AJ, Kevin got up and put a record on one of the turntables. It was a bouncy eighties electro song with a happy synth line that didn't match Ciara's mood at all. She wished she could ask him to turn it off, but Kevin had his back to her and was messing around with the record, scratching it back and forth.

"I asked Heidi if she liked you," Ciara said, desperate to break through to Kevin. "She said only as a friend."

"Oh, well." Kevin shrugged. She wished he would look at her. "We can't always get what we want."

"But we've been trying to land AJ and Heidi for weeks now!" Ciara shouted, jumping to her feet and going to stand next to him by the turntables. For some reason, it seemed very important to get him to look at her. Why was he acting so weird? "We had a whole plan and an operation with a special name and everything, and it totally blew up in our faces. Shouldn't you be more upset?"

She didn't know what she wanted from Kevin. Tears? Throwing things against the wall? She at least wanted him to mirror the way she felt—which was all dried up and useless and rotten on the inside. She was the one thing she hated to be most in the world: a failure.

"Look." Kevin finally turned and looked at her, and just being able to make eye contact made the tension in her shoulders release a little. "It didn't work out, okay? If they liked us, they'd be with us by now. So I'm just going to let what happens happen. Maybe you should try and go with the flow a little too."

"But we worked so hard," Ciara said. She knew she was whining. She heard Kevin's words and knew they probably made sense, but she just couldn't get them to penetrate her brain.

"Ciara." Kevin placed a comforting hand on her shoulder. "Just chill. Everything's going to be fine."

"All right," she said quietly. His eyes held hers, and his hand felt solid and warm. She wished she could just stay there for the rest of the day, safe in his studio with the rest of the world far away. The moment stretched out, and she felt the same tiny spark that had been there that night on the party boat when they had almost kissed.

"Things are going to be okay," Kevin said, giving her shoulder a friendly pat. "Really. I know you're probably freaked out about meeting your mom later, but it's going to be fine."

"Thanks," Ciara said gratefully. Once again, Kevin had managed to cut right through to what was really bothering her. Without thinking, she threw her arms around his waist and gave him a hug. She felt the uncertainty in his back for a moment before he wrapped his arms around her and hugged her tightly too, and then she closed her eyes and just let herself be next to him, smelling his clean, just-showered smell and luxuriating in the softness of his T-shirt against her cheek, his chest solid and strong.

Kevin let go just as she was starting to really feel relaxed. "What time do you have to meet your mom?" he asked.

Ciara opened her eyes, trying to ignore the sudden dizzy feeling in her head. "Soon," she said, checking her watch. "I should probably get going."

"All right," Kevin said. He quickly turned back to the turntables. "Good luck."

"I'll need it," Ciara muttered. She fought the urge to run over to him and beg for another hug, telling herself she must be feeling really vulnerable. It was probably just some weird reaction to getting rejected by AJ and having to face her mom in the same day: some shadow of the old Ciara who dealt with uncertainty by hooking up with the nearest guy. She told herself it was a good thing she was leaving before she did something she'd really regret.

"You'll be fine," Kevin said again. He flipped the record over and began playing the B side as she trudged up the stairs away from his studio and into the unforgivingly bright California day.

*   *   *

Her mom had made plans for them to meet at a quaint French bistro on Anapuma Street. Ciara felt anxiety squeezing her stomach into knots as she navigated the car down the twisting streets to Santa Barbara's quaint downtown. She hadn't seen her mom since the beginning of the summer, and so much had changed since then. At every stoplight, she wished she could turn the car around and go back home, crawl into bed, and sleep until fall. But then what? Was there any point in staying in Santa Barbara after everything that had just gone down? Things obviously weren't going to work out with AJ the way she'd planned, and if Heidi found out about Operation Woo-ha, she was in danger of losing one of her only girlfriends. Just thinking of returning to LA and Em's land of happy couplehood made her stomach turn. She felt like she had nowhere to go. And on top of all that, she had to go face her mom. What would she say?

She tried to brush away the nagging doubts as she made her way downtown, parked in the big municipal garage shaped like a bullring, and tugged at her shirt, trying to make the buttons lie flat across her chest. As she headed toward the restaurant, she whispered a plea to make the meal pleasant and drama free.

*   *   *

Her mom was sitting at a table by the window, sipping a club soda with lime. Ciara was exactly on time, so her mom must have arrived early. Typical—an overachiever in everything she did.

Her face lit up in a smile as Ciara entered the restaurant. She stood and gave her a huge hug, wrapping her arms so tightly around her daughter's waist that Ciara thought she was going to pass out.

"It's so good to see you!" she said as they sat down across from each other. Ciara was surprised to see the tiny network of wrinkles that had appeared around her mom's eyes and forehead—had those always been there? And what about the slight bags under her eyes? Her mom had always prided herself on her young-looking complexion. Her hair was an aggressive shade of black, much darker than usual, so that Ciara knew she had dyed it recently to cover up the gray. Was the divorce really taking *that* much of a toll on her, or was she just busy with work like always?

Ciara looked around for a waiter. She was tired and thirsty and dying for a Diet Coke. "It's good to see you too, Mom," she lied. "How are things?"

"Okay." Her voice faltered, making Ciara think that maybe things weren't really okay at all. She hoped her mom wouldn't go into it. The last thing she needed was more drama in her life. But her mother forced a smile and soldiered on. "Pretty busy. Packing up the house and moving is taking up a lot of time. I set aside a few boxes of your old toys and books, and I want you to go through them when you come home and let me know if there's anything you want to keep. We can give the rest away to Goodwill."

"Okay," Ciara said blankly. The phrase *when you come home* bounced around inside her head. A new house in LA wouldn't feel like home. Should she tell her mom about her plans to stay in Santa Barbara? Were those even still her plans?

"Plus, I'm thinking of switching ad agencies," her mom continued. She looked down at the table and toyed with her fork, using it to rake tiny furrows in her napkin.

"Really?" Ciara asked. She knew it was common to move around a lot in the advertising world, but her mom had been with the same agency since Ciara was in the sixth grade. "Why?"

"There have been some . . . internal complications, and I think I'd be happier somewhere else." Ciara wondered if it had anything to do with Clyde, the coworker with whom she'd had the affair. Had people found out? Did he change agencies too? Her mom sighed. "It's weird not having your dad to talk to about work stuff anymore," she said. "He always used to help me figure things out when I had to make tough decisions."

Ciara felt herself starting to get mad. Her mom was clearly the one who had ruined the relationship—she had no right to get all nostalgic over how wonderful her husband was. She grunted a neutral response to mask her anger.

The waiter came, and her mom ordered gratefully, clearly happy at the interruption. When he was gone, she turned to Ciara. "And how are you?" she asked.

"Oh, fine," Ciara said, trying to keep her tone light and focus on the positive. She told her mom all about her job at the beach club and the new friends she'd made, even adding that she was helping with marketing for a popular local band. The whole time, she couldn't help turning over her mom's comment about not having Dad in her life anymore. If she cared about him so much, why would she have done what she did?

No drama, she reminded herself as the waiter arrived with their food. Instead of talking about her relentless pursuit of AJ, she launched into the requirements of the prelaw programs she'd been researching on the Internet.

Her mom smiled proudly. "You remind me so much of me when I was your age," she said. "Always so driven and focused on making it. You know, that's part of the reason I married your father—he understood that my career always came first."

There she went: reminiscing about Ciara's dad again as if she hadn't stomped all over his heart in steel-toed boots. The gall made Ciara almost sick to her stomach. She quickly put down her forkful of blackened string beans and made herself take a deep breath before slowly sipping water. She couldn't even look at her mom for fear she'd explode and start screaming at her across the table.

"He was always so supportive," her mom mused. "You know, you're very lucky to have him as a father."

That did it. "If he's so great, why'd you dump him for someone else?" Ciara snapped before she could stop herself.

Her mom's face went white. "What are you talking about?" she asked. She brought her hand to her mouth and began chewing on the skin around one well-mani-cured nail.

"Oh, come on, Mom." Ciara gave her mother a glare full of all the rage she'd been storing up since she'd found out about the divorce: rage that up until then, she'd barely even let herself have. "I know about Clyde, okay? I heard both you and Dad mention it on the phone to your lawyers."

She watched her mom's face get even paler, but she was too angry to stop herself. "If you had to be so low and sneaky that you went creeping around behind Dad's back, you have no right to talk about how great he was like this divorce was some big mutual thing."

"It *was* a mutual thing," her mom whispered. She gripped the edge of the table with both hands as if trying to steady herself.

"Yeah, sure it was," Ciara spat. "You cheated on him. Real mutual, Mom."

"Your dad forgave me for Clyde," her mom croaked. She took a deep breath and continued. "But he said he could never trust me again, and if he couldn't trust me, we couldn't remain married. And I realized that I'd relied on him for so much of my life, I never had the chance to become my own person."

"And the way you became your own person was by sleeping around?" Ciara asked, slitting her eyes.

"Ciara!" Her mom's loud, shaky voice caused several other diners to jerk their heads in their direction. Ciara ducked her head in embarrassment. So much for no drama.

"How dare you accuse me of sleeping around," her mom continued in a lower tone that contained no less venom. "I had relations with one person besides your father."

"I can't believe you're still talking about it like it wasn't your fault!" Ciara hurled the words at her mother before she had a chance to screen them on their way out of her mouth. "It wasn't some unnatural force of evil that destroyed your marriage. *You* did. Everything was fine until you had to go and get it on with Clyde, and now I don't have a real family anymore."

"You still have a family." Tears gathered in her mom's eyes, and she tried to reach across the table and take Ciara's hand in hers, but Ciara jerked her hand away and shook her head. "Just because your father and I aren't married anymore doesn't mean we don't love you."

"Thanks for reading the pop psychology manual on talking to your kids about divorce," Ciara snapped. She was disgusted. All she wanted was for her mom to take responsibility for her actions. No, scratch that—all she *really* wanted was for her mom to have never done any of it in the first place.

"I mean it," her mom said, bringing her other hand to her mouth and nibbling on the skin around her pinkie nail.

Ciara wasn't in the mood for platitudes. She leaned back in her chair, away from her mom. "So I think I'm going to stay in Santa Barbara this fall instead of coming back to LA," she said, the way she might have said she thought she was going to have the key lime tart for dessert instead of the chocolate-cream pie.

Her mom practically spit out her club soda. Her face turned red as she brought her napkin to her lips, coughing into it.

"What do you mean, you're staying in Santa Barbara this fall?" she gasped.

Ciara shrugged. She hadn't even meant to tell her mom about her plans—if they were even still plans—but the whole conversation made her so mad she wanted something to throw back in her mom's face. Something that would finally get it through her head that Ciara wasn't some dumb little kid who could be lied to and then quickly smoothed over with a kind word or two. "Dad lives here now, and there's plenty of room for me in the house," she said. "Plus, I have friends here, and the public schools are excellent, so you wouldn't have to pay for tuition at Westwood anymore."

"But I already put down the deposit!" Her mom looked like she was drowning. "And I've painted your bedroom, and what about the debate club, and won't Em miss you, and . . ."

"Those are just details, Mom," Ciara said coldly. She took the napkin off her lap and folded it neatly on the table. "And maybe you should have thought of those before you took up with Clyde. Because you know what? When you cheated on Dad, it wasn't just him you screwed over. It was me too."

Ciara felt so calm she was almost shaking. Without another word, she stood up and walked out of the restaurant.

Chapter Sixteen

Wear clean drawers every day
'Cuz things may fall the wrong way

— *The Coup*

Ciara drove aimlessly up and down the streets of Santa Barbara for a while, watching the wealthy summer people promenade up and down the well-kept main street with its white-and-peach Spanish stucco specialty shops and neatly coiffed palm trees. She could hardly believe she'd just walked out on her mom like that. On one hand, it had felt good to tell her how she felt after over a month of polite phone conversation. On the other, she felt kind of bad that she'd hurt her mom's feelings.

Feeling aimless and discouraged, she drove down to the beach and pulled into the parking lot by the skate park. Thin, serious-looking boys with long yellow hair peeking out from under their helmets poised at the top of the quarter pipe, their mouths set in hard determination in the moment before they went flying down the pipe, soaring up again on the other side, sometimes crashing in the middle with their boards on top of them. She wished she had something to do with the rest of her day or at least someone to talk to.

She pulled out her phone and called Kevin, remembering how calm his hand on her shoulder had made her feel earlier that morning. Kevin had been through his parents getting a divorce—he would understand. Maybe he'd even have some good advice for her.

It took Kevin a long time to pick up, but he answered just as she'd resigned herself to talking to his voice mail.

"Hey," he said, his voice deep and comforting. "How was lunch?"

Ciara suddenly found herself not wanting to talk about it. The gray sky made her feel listless and frustrated.

"It was fine," she said simply. "I'm bored. Want to hang out or something?"

There was a long pause on the other end of the line. "Uh, I'm kind of chilling with Marlene right now," Kevin said finally. "Is it okay if I call you later?"

Ciara said it was fine, even though she sort of felt like it wasn't. As she hung up and watched a tubby middle school guy try to flip an ollie, she realized it was the first time all summer Kevin had blown her off. Maybe now that they didn't have Operation Woo-ha, she didn't matter to him as much anymore. The thought made her inexplicably blue. She tried to tell herself that she didn't need him as much, either, but even the stern voice inside her head didn't sound very convincing. She pictured Marlene in Kevin's studio, sitting on the floor next to him as they listened to record after record, their knees bumping as they talked and laughed. The image made her chest tight and achy. Why couldn't Kevin hang out with her and Marlene at the same time? Something *must* be going on between them!

She realized she was breathing heavily, and her cheeks felt hot as she walked away from the skate park and toward the pier, the briny smell of the ocean so strong it was almost suffocating. Three young girls strolled by her, laughing as they licked at dripping ice-cream cones. She fought pangs of jealousy, wishing she had someone to spend the afternoon with. Of course, she could always call Heidi, but something told her that dealing with Heidi's grief over AJ would only make her more depressed. Instead, she sat down on a bench and watched the wind whip the ocean's surface into tiny white-tipped wavelets. A seagull perched on the rail in front of her and looked at her accusingly.

"What?" she asked it out loud.

The seagull cocked its head, as if to say, "You *know* what."

Her cell phone buzzed, startling the seagull so that it flew away. Ciara's heart leaped in her chest. Maybe Kevin had changed his mind! She knew that just spending a few hours with him would make her feel better. But when she flipped it open to check the text, she was stunned to see that it wasn't Kevin at all.

It was AJ.

What's going on? it said.

Ciara couldn't help thinking that was a damn good question. What *was* going on? Why was AJ texting her the day after more or less dumping her the moment she'd shown him how she really felt? Did he mean "what's going on" as in "what are you up to today?" or "what's going on with *us*?" And why was she disappointed that the text was from him instead of Kevin? Why was Kevin suddenly the only thing on her mind?

Should she text AJ back right away? Wait a while so she wouldn't seem all desperate? Why did a simple text message have the power to plummet her into the throes of confusion? That was the problem with text messages—the lack of context was enough to drive anyone nuts.

Loneliness and curiosity won out over not seeming desperate, and she texted him back: *Not much. Bored. What r u up to?*

She wandered over to one of the cheesy souvenir shops while waiting for him to text her back. A rack of mini California license plates stared up at her, and she idly spun it to the *C*s, looking for her name. A T-shirt with *Santa Barbara* written across the front in colorful graffiti script caught her eye, and she thought briefly about getting it for Kevin—he would get a kick out of how tacky it was.

Stop thinking about Kevin! she admonished herself. But she couldn't. Her thoughts returned obsessively to the hug they'd shared earlier that morning, replaying it from a million different angles. What had it meant . . . and why had it meant so much?

AJ finally texted back, inviting her over. Well, why not? She had nothing better to do. She considered running home and changing out of her conservative lunch-with-mom clothes and into something sexier—the kind of thing that would make AJ sit up and take notice—but then decided not to bother. He'd already more or less said he wasn't into her, so why keep trying? It was time to bury Operation Woo-ha as far in the recesses of her mind as it would go.

*   *   *

When she got to AJ's place, he was sitting on his bed, listening to a recording of his last practice session with the B-Dizzy Crew and looking over a bunch of papers spread out over the covers.

"Hey, AJ." She sat down on the edge of his bed. "How's it going?"

"Great. I was just looking at these drafts of our logo. Which one do you like?"

Ciara leaned over to get a better look. Her head was now just inches from his, and his musky smell was starting to affect her. Why did she have to be so attracted to him? It was unfair. Her brain was telling her to just call it quits and accept that they would only ever be friends, but the way her pulse raced and her skin heated up when she was around him said something else entirely. She wondered idly if it was really anything more than pure lust.

"I like this one," she said, picking up a page that had the crew's name written in shaky, angular blue graffiti print with green lines around it. "The lines make it look kind of techie—like you're on the cutting edge."

AJ grinned, showing off his dimples. "I think that's my favorite too," he said. "But then again, I really like this one." He held up a page where the letters were all on different levels, making the logo look kind of disoriented.

"It's a little hard to read," Ciara said dubiously. She was having trouble concentrating on the logos. All she could think about was what had happened the night before. Their kiss and subsequent conversation hung in the air like an invisible question mark; everything about the two of them being together felt different to her, but AJ seemed oblivious. He was going on and on about the image he wanted to create for the group, how he wanted to be seen as hard-core but also kind of playful at the same time, kind of like A Tribe Called Quest in the early days, and Ciara felt herself tuning in and out as he spoke. She watched his thick, full lips move up and down while he talked and couldn't help thinking she wanted those lips to kiss her again. How many times over the summer had she been distracted from what AJ was saying by how hot he was? And why was the thought of kissing suddenly making her think of Kevin?

She realized AJ was looking at her expectantly. He'd asked a question, and she had missed it.

"What?" she asked dumbly.

"I asked if you wanted to go to the mall," AJ said. "I want to pick up the new 50 Cent album."

"Oh," Ciara said, coming out of her haze. "Sure."

Maybe being in public would make her less loopy. As it was, she couldn't help thinking that here they were alone in his bedroom with his parents not home . . .

sitting on his *bed*, for goodness sake. No wonder she was getting worked up. Given her past, it would be a dangerous situation with anyone, let alone a guy as hot as AJ.

*　　*　　*

In the car, AJ plugged in his iPod and tuned it to yet another practice session recording of the B-Dizzy Crew.

"What do you think of this song?" he asked. Ciara listened to his voice coming through the speakers. To be honest, it wasn't the most original song she'd ever heard.

"It's good," she said diplomatically. "But maybe the lyrics could use a little spicing up. I mean, you basically just repeat the same line over and over again."

She could almost see the hairs on the back of AJ's neck bristle. "You don't like it?" he asked.

"I didn't say that!" Ciara assured him. "I just think there's room for improvement. I mean, you want to be the best, right?"

"Yeah . . . ," AJ said reluctantly. "But I thought that song was really good."

Ciara shrugged. Why was he having so much trouble taking a little criticism? If he wanted to make it big, he would probably have to endure a whole lot more of it. "So add some more words," she said. "I mean, that line is catchy and people can sing along to it, but maybe you should have a verse or two explaining what you're talking about. I mean, you say 'da girl looks good, da girl looks fine, gonna make her mine.' Maybe you could say what girl, or why you like her so much, or what it is that makes her look good. Like, describe her a little. Talk about the situation. You know, build some narrative."

AJ looked confused, and Ciara gave up. She stared out the window and watched the scenery roll by until they got to the mall. As they entered the double doors leading to the glassed-in atrium, a group of girls stared openly at AJ before turning to each other and whispering in hushed, excited voices. AJ gave her a helpless shrug, and Ciara felt her annoyance increase. No wonder Marlene was always harping on AJ's ego—it really did start to get on your nerves after a while.

Thinking of Marlene made her think of Kevin, which made her chest tighten again. She wondered what the two of them were doing right then. She hoped it was something really innocuous and preferably with a lot of other people around.

"Hey, chill," AJ said. "You look like you're about to bite someone's head off. I didn't even say hi to those girls!"

It took Ciara a moment to realize what he was talking about, and she almost laughed when she did. As usual, AJ thought that everything in the world had to do with him. Although, come to think of it, for most of the summer she'd thought so too.

The new 50 Cent album was playing over the speakers in the music store, and kids in bright, clean clothes flipped through racks of CDs or listened to music through headphones, bobbing their heads up and down to their own private beats.

"All right!" AJ said excitedly. "This tune is pumping!"

The pixie-like girl at the counter flipped her platinum-streaked hair over her shoulder and shot AJ a coy smile as he walked in.

"Maybe they'll be playing my tunes in here someday," he said to Ciara, loud enough for the pixie to hear. He picked up the CD from the Hot Picks rack in the front of the store, and Ciara wandered over to the hip-hop section to see if they had the J-Live album that Kevin had played for her recently. AJ followed her, asking what she was looking for.

"Oh, that guy's amazing," he said when she told him. "Did you know he DJs and emcees at the same time? I could never do that."

"It's gotta be incredibly hard," Ciara agreed. "And did you know he's also an inner-city public school teacher?"

"Talk about an overachiever." AJ laughed.

They spent a long time looking over the CDs in the hip-hop section, talking about their favorite artists and which groups never should have recorded albums in the first place. Ciara was starting to relax. This was how she liked things to be with AJ: easy and fun, without any drama. Her favorite thing about hanging out with him was just shooting the breeze and talking about music and laughing.

"So, you *just* wanted to stop in and get the new 50 Cent CD, huh?" Ciara joked as they strolled out of the store together.

"No more Frappuccinos for me this summer." AJ groaned. "I just spent almost a hundred bucks." He glanced inside the big yellow bag from the music store, which was stuffed with CDs.

"Please," Ciara scoffed. "Which is more important—coffee or music?"

AJ laughed and draped his arm over her shoulders. "That's what I like about you," he said easily as they strolled toward the food court. "You got your priorities straight."

There it was—his arm over her shoulders, warm and heavy and hyper-real. With her arm still down at her side, it bumped awkwardly against his hip, so she wrapped it around his waist. She tried to pretend to herself that it was no big deal—they were just friends walking through the mall with their arms around each other. But why did he keep sending her mixed messages?

Either he liked her or he didn't . . . which meant that either he wanted to touch her or he didn't. The fact that he couldn't be clear with her was starting to get on her nerves.

She looked up at him, hoping to see some kind of sign in his eyes. Was that smile he was giving her suggestive and loaded with longing and hidden meaning or just a regular old grin because she'd said something funny? It was hard to tell with AJ. It was almost like he wanted to keep things ambiguous—and he was so cute, it clouded her powers of deductive reasoning.

"You know, sometimes I feel like you're sending me mixed signals," she murmured as AJ nuzzled his cheek against her hair. It was the kind of gesture you usually saw a guy doing when he'd been dating someone a long time, not when he'd just rejected her the night before. She felt like she had a right to be confused.

"Yeah, sorry," AJ said. He stopped walking and turned to her, putting both hands on her shoulders and looking deep into her eyes. "Seriously, I feel bad about last night. I'm just confused about who I really want to be with."

A burst of mall traffic brushed past them, forcing them so close together that Ciara could feel his breath on her cheek. She felt dizzy and hot, like she'd been stuck in a car without AC on the freeway during rush-hour traffic. Did AJ mean he actually *did* want to be with her? And if so, did she still feel the same way? It seemed like there wasn't enough oxygen in the air, and she found herself trying to breathe quietly to mask the fact that she was almost panting.

"I think you're really fly, Ciara," he said, his face inches from hers. "You're smart and cool and sexy. But—"

"What the heck is going *on* here?!" a voice shrieked inches from Ciara's face. She and AJ whirled to find Heidi in a Juicy tank top and cutoffs, carrying a jumbo-sized Berry Blast smoothie and wearing an expression that was very sad, very angry, and very confused all at the same time.

"Oh, hey, Heidi," Ciara said, quickly unwrapping her arm from AJ's waist. Guilt throbbed through her veins and turned her face scarlet. Her voice sounded as fake enthusiastic as a camp counselor's who'd just been assigned to clean up the puke in the dining hall. "Uh . . . what's up?"

"What's *up*?!" Heidi shrieked as if it were the most ludicrous question in the world. "What do you mean, what's *up*? I go to the mall for a little retail therapy after a rough night, and I find my friend practically sucking face with the guy who dumped me less than twenty-four hours ago. I don't know, Ciara—maybe you better tell *me* what's up."

"Hey, this isn't what it looks like," AJ began.

"Well, what is it?" Heidi looked angrily from him to Ciara. "Because it looks to me like you guys were just getting cozy in the middle of the freakin' mall." Her chin quivered as she continued her tirade. "I thought we were friends, Ciara. I trusted you. Were you just after AJ this whole time? Because if you were, that is *low*."

Ciara was too stunned to come up with a good lie. "I'm sorry," she said quietly. She couldn't look Heidi in the eye. Instead, she stared down at the dirt wedged in the cracks between the mall's terra-cotta-tiled floor. "I just thought we'd be so perfect together. I didn't mean to hurt you."

"You sure screwed *that* up!" Heidi screamed. She turned and ran away from them, her flip-flops slapping against the floor. Groups of girls with their lips glossed slicker than the surface of a mirror swiveled their heads to watch her, then turned back to each other to speculate in loud whispers. The farther away Heidi got from them, the lower Ciara's spirits sank. She really hadn't meant to hurt Heidi, but the truth was, she hadn't been thinking. She'd been so hell-bent on getting AJ as a boyfriend that she hadn't considered anyone's feelings but her own.

And now not only was AJ not her boyfriend, but Heidi wasn't her friend anymore, either. The funny thing was, she was almost more upset about the latter. She'd thought losing AJ had been a blow, but knowing that Heidi was mad at her hurt even more. She turned to AJ and sighed.

"I feel awful," she said bluntly.

AJ looked at her, surprised. "Have you really been after me all summer?" he asked. His eyes were wide with curiosity, and Ciara felt a tiny twinge of resentment. She felt so bad about Heidi, and here AJ was turning the conversation back to himself.

Ciara decided to ignore his question. "How long do you think she'll stay mad at me?" she asked. "What can I do to make things better?"

"Oh, I don't know," AJ said. "I'm sure she'll be fine. Maybe I'll give her a call and let her know I still care about her as a friend."

"But it's not *about* you and Heidi!" Ciara said. "It's about Heidi and *me*! *I'm* the one who screwed up and hurt her feelings, and I'm the one who needs to make things better. It has nothing to do with you."

AJ looked confused. "But it *was* about me," he said. "You guys were just fighting over me. I was standing right here. I saw you."

Ciara scanned his face for signs he was joking, but he seemed totally serious. He didn't even seem to care that two of his friends were fighting. What mattered to him was that they were fighting over *him*.

Ciara suddenly realized where all of Marlene's comments about AJ's ego had come from. He really *was* sort of self-centered. She'd just been too busy idolizing him to notice.

"Whatever." She sighed. She wondered if she should go after Heidi, but it already seemed too late. She'd have to work on figuring out the perfect way to win her back as a friend.

AJ draped his arm over her shoulders again. Ciara waited for the tingle she always got when he touched her, but this time, it didn't come. "Don't worry," he said. "Things will work out." The words sounded less comforting and genuine coming from AJ than they had from Kevin earlier that day.

"I hope so." Ciara sighed again. "I really, really hope so."

Chapter Seventeen

Da girl looks good, da girl looks fine
Gonna make her mine

—The B-Dizzy Crew

"Hey, I have a text message!" AJ announced as they left the mall and walked through the parking lot toward his car. He dug in his low-slung jeans for his phone and flipped it open. "Oh, sweet, it's D-John. He's having people over to swim. Want to head over there?"

"Sure." Ciara shrugged. She didn't want to go swim at D-John's. At the same time, there was nothing else she wanted to do, either. Maybe being around people would keep her from moping. Or maybe someone would have the answer to all her problems and would help magically solve them all within a half hour like in a sitcom.

Yeah, right. And maybe Paris Hilton would get her act together and settle down with someone who wasn't a Greek millionaire and get a nine-to-five job.

"I'll go, but I won't have my suit," she said.

"There's always underwear," AJ joked. Ciara just rolled her eyes.

In the car on the way over, AJ put on the 50 Cent CD and turned the volume way up, swaying slightly to the beat.

"Man, I would love to be as famous as this guy," he said. "Can you imagine? Private jets, limos, designers fighting each other to give you top-dollar clothes for free. And everyone dressing like you, talking like you, rushing out to buy your album the moment it comes out. I want *that*."

"I thought you just wanted to make music," Ciara said grumpily.

AJ gave her a look that said, *What crawled up your butt and died?* But he kept his tone of voice light. "Well, of course I want that too," he said. "But I don't *just* want to make music. I want to make music that everyone loves."

By the time they got to D-John's, Ciara's guilt had settled into a full-on funk. All she could think about was the expression on Heidi's face when she'd said, *I thought we were friends.*

As if to mock her, the weather had turned beautiful while they were in the mall. The sun shone with renewed intensity, the sky gleamed a sapphire blue, and a fresh breeze wafted up from the ocean and into the hills, tempering the warmth of the sun. Birds chirped merrily in the trees around D-John's compound, and she could already hear the bubbling laughter of people splashing around in the pool. The scene that awaited her when they turned the corner of the house was like some-thing out of a soda commercial: girls in bikinis and guys in baggy swim shorts playing water volleyball, grilling burgers, drinking soda, and laughing at everything. The atmosphere was pure party—exactly the opposite of the static in her head.

"Hey, man," D-John said, slapping AJ five. "Glad you could make it. I have this sweet new mixer you gotta check out."

D-John led AJ into the house, and Ciara deliberately wandered away from them and over toward the tables and chairs clustered by the pool. She was surprised to see Kevin there, sitting on a bench . . . with Marlene.

A weird little contraction pulsed in Ciara's stomach, and her mood dipped even lower than before. What was going on? Seeing Kevin should have made her happy, but instead she wanted to cry. She wanted to talk to Kevin more than ever—he would know what to do about Heidi. He always seemed to have the answer; it was one of the things she liked best about him. But of course, she couldn't be open with him about the whole situation with Marlene there. Ciara started to turn away from them, but it was too late. Kevin and Marlene were already calling her name and waving her over.

She approached reluctantly. She could probably fake a good mood with Marlene, but she knew Kevin would see right through her. What would he say if he knew what she was really feeling? She wasn't sure she could handle being rejected again.

Ciara arranged her mouth into what she knew must look like a ridiculous excuse for a smile and joined them at one of the wrought-iron tables.

Sure enough, Kevin took one look at her and asked what was wrong.

"Nothing," Ciara said, dropping the stupid smile. "I'm just a little tired. That's all."

"Is it your mom?" Kevin asked.

Ciara squirmed in her seat. She didn't want to talk about it in front of Marlene. Besides, so much had happened since she'd left her mom sitting alone at that table in the French restaurant that it felt like a million years ago.

"Never mind," Kevin said. "We don't have to talk about it. It's a beautiful day today, huh?"

It would be more beautiful if I could enjoy it alone with you. The thought entered Ciara's mind with such force that she didn't have time to push it out again. It gelled in her head, pushing out all the noise and static. She wanted Kevin! Images from the summer flashed in front of her like a slide show: Kevin sitting next to her at Six Flags, working the turntables on the party boat, looking into her eyes with his hand on her shoulder that very morning. He had been there all along, but she'd been too dumb to even realize it . . . and now it was probably too late.

"Ciara?" He repeated her name gently.

"Yeah," she said lamely. "Nice day."

"So I noticed you showed up with AJ," Kevin said. To anyone else, the question would have sounded merely conversational, but Ciara knew it was loaded with meaning.

"Yeah, we were hanging out," she said vaguely. If Kevin wanted to "hang out" with Marlene all day, why shouldn't she "hang out" with AJ too?

"Yeah?" Kevin asked, his eyes narrowed. "What were you guys doing before you came here?"

"Jeez, Kevin—what is this, the Spanish Inquisition?" Marlene laughed. "They were hanging out, okay? I'm sure if they had been off robbing little old ladies, you'd be the first to know."

"You're right." Kevin's eyes unslitted, but he still looked unsettled. "Sorry. It's none of my business."

"No, that's cool," Ciara said breezily. It made her happy that Kevin cared even a little about what AJ had been up to. It almost eclipsed her mad jealousy of Marlene. "We were just buying CDs at the mall. We ran into Heidi there."

Kevin's eyes practically bugged out of his head. Ciara could tell he was dying to know what had happened. It felt good not to tell him.

"That's weird—I called and invited her here earlier, and she said she didn't feel up to it," Marlene interjected. "I told her that you and AJ would probably drop by too. I can't imagine why she didn't want to come."

Ciara slid her eyes over to Kevin. He raised his eyebrow slightly at her. *They* could certainly imagine why Heidi wouldn't have wanted to come!

"She said she wasn't feeling that great," Ciara lied. "She was on her way home when I ran into her."

"Oh, maybe I should call her and make sure she's okay," Marlene volunteered. She began to dig in her purse for her phone. Ciara began to panic.

"I think she said she was going to take a nap!" she said quickly.

"Oh." Marlene shrugged and returned her phone to her bag. "I don't want to wake her up. Guess I'll just call later."

AJ emerged from the house, rolling his shoulders so he looked even taller and stronger than usual and squinting in the bright afternoon sunlight. He put his hand over his eyes to shade them as he scanned the crowd, spotted her, and waved before heading over. As he approached, he noticed Kevin and Marlene and slowed down a bit, his movements suddenly uncertain.

"Hey." He nodded at Ciara and Kevin, keeping his gaze on Marlene as he sprawled out in a lounge chair. "I just checked out D-John's new mixer. It's pretty sweet."

"Yeah—I can't believe his parents got him an eight channel," Kevin agreed. "I'd have to work for months to afford one of those—and D-John barely ever even spins in public. He just messes around in his room."

"Not everyone's as serious about achieving fame and fortune as we are." AJ shrugged.

Kevin looked pained. "It's not fame and fortune I'm serious about," he said. "It's music."

"Well, duh, that too!" AJ said. He looked from Kevin to Ciara to Marlene. "Jeez, what is with you guys today? Did I forget to mark Attack AJ Day on my calendar or something?"

Marlene shrugged and gave him an impish smile, which made AJ shift in his chair and look down at the flagstone tiles around the pool. "Anyway," he continued. "Kevin, I'm glad you're here. I wanted to talk about getting matching jerseys for the Coup show. Plus, I brought mock-ups of some of the ideas for the logos. . . ."

He began digging in his pants pockets for the colored slips of paper, and Ciara stopped listening. She looked over at Marlene, who rolled her eyes and mouthed, "Here we go again." Ciara cracked a sympathetic smile in response. No wonder Marlene had broken up with AJ—he really was obsessed with polishing the B-Dizzy Crew's image so they could get famous. It was good to be goal-oriented, but not to the exclusion of everything else. AJ was so bent on fame and fortune, he seemed to have forgotten all about his friends.

As AJ talked on and on about the visual picture he wanted them to create onstage, Ciara tried to catch Kevin's eye. If only the two of them could talk in private, she bet they would be able to come up with some brilliant scheme for her to win Heidi back as a friend. But Kevin's attention seemed equally divided between listening to AJ and sharing knowing looks with Marlene. In the meantime, AJ seemed distracted. He kept trailing off in the middle of sentences, glancing uneasily at Kevin and Marlene sitting on the bench together and then launching back into the conversation with twice the energy, talking a mile a minute. Ciara wondered if it bothered him that Kevin was maybe-kinda-probably hooking up with Marlene. After all, they hadn't broken up that long ago. Even Marlene, who always seemed comfortable in every situation, kept looking up at the sky as if she wished she were somewhere else.

Ciara gave up trying to get Kevin's attention. The whole scene was just really awkward. With everyone in the same group of two guys and three girls always crushing on each other and hitting on each other and dating and scheming and hooking up and breaking up, her life was starting to seem like the 24/7 Drama Channel: All Drama, All the Time. And she hated it. She wished they could all just be friends like they had been back in the beach club days when they were thirteen, when Kevin and AJ were still Star Wars nerds and she, Heidi, and Marlene were more concerned with who could do the most underwater somersaults than who could get the hottest guy.

Ciara stood up, stretched her arms over her head, and made her way to the diving board at the deep end of the pool. She could feel AJ, Kevin, and Marlene staring at her back, but she didn't turn around. She stepped out onto the diving board, bounced lightly up and down, and then dove in.

Cool blue water enveloped her head, and she opened her eyes to the sting of chlorine. Down at the shallow end, she could see legs waving, the flickering reds and oranges of bathing suit bottoms darting back and forth.

She turned around and swam in the other direction with long, forceful strokes.

Everything began to fall into place. She'd spent the whole summer chasing a dream that was just that: a dream. The AJ she'd wanted wasn't AJ the person; it was AJ the image of the ideal boyfriend. Marlene knew what AJ the person was like, and she'd dumped him when he got too self-centered. But if AJ the person was so goal-oriented that he forgot his friends, then she was twice as bad. Look what she'd done to Heidi, who had been nothing but nice to her ever since she arrived, who had gotten her a job, invited her out, confided in her, and made sure she felt included in the group. All summer long, Ciara had thought that making AJ her boyfriend was the only way to get out of the rut she'd created for herself back in LA—but maybe she needed to change more than just her single-girl status to become the person she really wanted to be.

Ciara knew what she had to do. She had to make everything right again, and she had to do it now, before the chance slipped away from her forever. She had wasted nearly the whole summer going after the wrong guy—she didn't have another moment to spare. She had to make things right with Heidi. Even if it was too late for her to win Kevin over, she could still fight to get Heidi back as a friend.

She climbed out of the water, grabbed a towel from the back of a chair next to her group of friends, and began drying off.

"Where are you going?" Kevin asked.

"I have to find Heidi," Ciara said, pulling her broomstick skirt on over her still-wet bikini bottom. "We have a lot of talking to do."

"I thought you said she was sick," Marlene said.

"I lied," Ciara said flatly. "She's mad at me, and I didn't want her telling you about it. I'm sorry."

"Oh." Marlene looked stricken. "Well, jeez. I hope you can work it out."

"I hope so too," Ciara said for the second time that day. "That's why I need to talk to her right away. Not being honest has gotten me into a lot of trouble this summer—it's time for me to come clean."

*　　*　　*

The sun was just beginning to dip toward the west as Ciara drove to Heidi's house, her heart pounding as she tried to work out the right thing to say.

"I'm sorry I hurt you," she said to the stoplight up ahead. "I was selfish and cruel, and I didn't think about the effect my actions would have. I know you must be very mad at me, and I will do anything I can to make it up to you. I hope that someday we can be friends again."

The stoplight turned green, which she took as a good sign, as if it were giving her the go-ahead not just in traffic, but in her friendship as well.

Lights blazed in the windows of Heidi's house as Ciara pulled into the driveway, and she could smell the rich garlicky scent of lasagna spilling out the kitchen window.

"Heidi's in her room," her mom said when Ciara stepped into the kitchen. She looked just like Ciara remembered her, although her hair was a bit shorter and flecked by more gray. "Should I tell her you're here?"

"If it's all right, I'd like to just go up," Ciara said. If Heidi's mom announced that she was here, Heidi might just ask her to tell Ciara to go away.

"Go on," her mom said warmly. "I'd ask you to stay for dinner, but I think Heidi's going out."

"That's cool." Ciara's heart beat faster as she headed slowly up the stairs. Was the speech she'd prepared dumb? Would Heidi forgive her? She could hear Kelly Clarkson blasting from Heidi's room—"Since U Been Gone." Heidi was singing along with feeling, and Ciara's stomach flopped. Was she singing about AJ—or her? She knocked lightly on the door.

"I'll be down in a minute, Mom!" Heidi called.

"Um, Heidi?" Ciara said. Her voice sounded shaky in her ears. "It's not your mom. It's me. Ciara."

"Go away!" Heidi screamed. "I don't want to talk to you, and I don't forgive you."

"Can we please talk?" Ciara couldn't believe she was begging, but she was. She told herself it was worth it.

"No!" Heidi yelled back. "I have a date with a cute guy tonight, and I don't want you stealing him too."

Ouch. That stung. A lot. She wondered if she should just turn around and go home—if Heidi was going to throw jabs like that at her, maybe she shouldn't even bother. But she reminded herself that Heidi had a right to be mad. If a friend had done to her what she did to Heidi, she'd be throwing barbs too.

Ciara took a deep breath. She had to keep trying. "Heidi, I'm really, really sorry," she called through the door. "I know I hurt you, and I didn't mean to. I just . . . I . . ."

She'd forgotten her speech. She felt a lump rise in her throat and begged herself not to cry. "I just want to keep being your friend," she said.

She wasn't even sure Heidi could hear her, but a moment later, the music stopped and the door opened. Heidi stared out at her, a scowl on her face. She had toned down the makeup and was wearing natural-looking eye shadow and a touch of lip gloss with a plain white turtleneck tank top and a hip pair of Seven jeans.

"Look, I'm still really mad at you, and I don't forgive you," Heidi said. "What you did was really slimy and underhanded, and I don't think I can trust you anymore."

"I know." Ciara looked down at the thick mauve carpeting on the hallway floor, unable to meet Heidi's eyes. "It's just . . . like, my parents just got a divorce and my mom was messing around and I've been trying to pretend it didn't bother me, but maybe it did more than I thought and now . . . well, I guess I've just been lashing out at everyone. Especially you. And I feel really bad, and I'm really sorry."

She got up the courage to look back from the floor and into Heidi's eyes, but Heidi didn't seem to have melted.

"You may want to take a look at yourself and see who you're really angry with," she said quietly. "Now, if you'll excuse me, I have to go meet someone."

She brushed past Ciara and trotted down the stairs, leaving Ciara staring at her retreating back. She gulped hard, trying to force back tears, before following Heidi down the steps and out the door. Heidi was already getting into her car.

"Don't you dare follow me," she said, starting up the engine. "All I want is for you to leave me alone."

"I'm sorry," Ciara said again, but Heidi had already backed out of the driveway and was driving down the street. Feeling more defeated than she ever had in her life, Ciara got in her car and sat taking deep breaths, trying to keep the tears at bay. Then she turned the key, swung out onto the quiet suburban street, and headed home.

Chapter Eighteen

When I cry, you cry, we cry together

—Ja Rule

Ciara was so hysterical by the time she got home that her breath was coming in ragged, uneven gasps. All she wanted was to lock herself in her room, listen to something sad and slow like Norah Jones, and crawl under the covers. She didn't care that it wasn't even nine yet—she was ready to go to sleep and forget everything. Maybe things would be better when she woke up. Somehow, she doubted it.

She was about to pull into the driveway when she noticed her mom's black Eclipse parked on the street in front of her house. Great—on top of everything else, her mom had come to find her and torment her more. Ciara considered turning around and driving somewhere else, but she was too emotionally beat to even know where to go. The front door felt like a thousand pounds as she pushed it open and followed the sound of her father's weary, serious voice to the kitchen. Two very familiar heads looked up at her, their voices suddenly shushed. Ciara realized with a start that it was the first time she had seen her parents in the same room in several months.

"Hi, Mom," Ciara said dully.

Her dad motioned for her to come and sit with them at the kitchen table. She suddenly felt the way she had when she was five years old and her parents came home from a movie to find the babysitter freaking out and Ciara drawing all over the walls with crayons. She reluctantly took a seat and looked from one parent to the other. This time, she saw the lines around both of their eyes, the ghosts of gray streaking through her dad's hair as well as the aggressive black covering her mom's aging roots. Both of them looked tired, confused, and sad.

"Ciara," her dad began. "Your mom says you told her today at lunch that you're planning on staying here in Santa Barbara this fall. Is that true?"

Ciara's head began to spin. She'd been so busy focusing on her love drama and friend drama, she'd practically forgotten about paying attention to her family drama as well. Now it was all blowing up in her face. There was no way they'd let her stay here. It was a dumb idea in the first place.

Besides, with the way things were going with her only friends in Santa Barbara, she wasn't even sure she *wanted* to stay. Things might be simpler if she just returned to LA and never had to face AJ, Heidi, Marlene, or Kevin ever again. At the same time, just the thought made her stomach hurt.

"I was thinking about it," she said lamely, looking at the wood grain on the tabletop.

"You never told me that," her father said.

"I wanted to surprise you." Her voice sounded very, very small.

"Well, you sure have done that," her dad said. "Listen, we want you to be happy. So if what you really want is to stay here with me, we'll give the matter very careful consideration."

"But I'll miss you a lot," her mom said wistfully.

"Well, maybe you should have thought of that before you betrayed my trust," Ciara countered.

Her mom gasped, then put her head in her hands and began crying softly. When she looked up again, her cheeks were streaked with mascara and tears. She wasn't beautiful or glamorous when she cried. She was just a woman whose own daughter didn't trust her anymore.

"And you." Ciara turned on her dad. "You divorced Mom because she cheated on you, but you told me it was because the two of you were just growing apart. Why didn't you tell the truth?"

Her father's face drooped. "I guess it's because we didn't want you putting all the blame on your mom," he said finally. "Truthfully, we really were growing apart. For several years now, we just didn't feel the same togetherness that we used to. You know we got married when we were very young. We had a rich life together for a long time, but after a while, it wasn't the same. We started wanting different things out of life, and we realized we weren't compatible anymore."

It was almost exactly what her mom had said at lunch. Still . . .

"That doesn't give you an excuse to cheat!" Ciara said to her mom.

"I know," her mom whimpered, wiping her eyes with the back of her hand.

Ciara looked wildly toward her dad, but he was shaking his head. "We just weren't happy together anymore," he said. "Your mom's affair was the catalyst we needed to let us know we had to end things."

"But how could you have hurt Dad like that?" Ciara asked, her voice rising until she sounded nearly hysterical. "There's no excusing or justifying that—it was just an awful, low, sleazy thing to do. How am I supposed to respect you after that?"

"Haven't you ever made a mistake?" her mom asked quietly through her tears. Then she got up, pushing her chair back so that it screeched unbearably on the tile floor, and ran toward the door.

"Maria, wait," her dad called, but the door had already swung shut. A moment later, they heard the car start up and her mom burning rubber, trying to get out of there as quickly as possible.

Ciara's heart sank. She hadn't meant to hurt her mom—and she hadn't meant to hurt Heidi, either. Her mom's words rang in her ears. Of course she had made mistakes. She'd made the biggest mistake of her life that very summer, screwing over her friend to try and get a guy. Even when you tried really hard and your intentions were good and you thought you were doing the right thing, it sometimes turned out to be wrong. That's what had happened with Operation Woo-ha. Maybe that was what had happened with her mother and Clyde too.

She took a deep breath. She didn't want to cry.

Her dad got up and came around to the chair next to her, pulling it up beside her and putting his arm over her shoulders. "What your mom did hurt everyone in this family, including her," he continued. "But I've forgiven her, and she's on the road to forgiving herself."

"Does that mean you're getting back together?" Ciara asked. To her shock, her voice was filled with hope. She had never been able to pretend, even to herself, that was what she really wanted. Suddenly, she realized that she wanted it more than anything. She would have given up all the boys in the world just to be a family again.

"I'm sorry, baby," her dad said quietly. His voice sounded choked as well. "That can't happen. There's too much water under the bridge for us to make it work. But we can still forgive each other and get on with our lives. And we can still admit that the people closest to us have the most power to hurt us—and that it's okay to admit that it hurts."

Ciara lost it. She was crying. Tears spilled out onto the coffee table, and her dad wordlessly handed her a napkin, which she quickly soaked.

"Shhh." He put his arms around her and rocked her gently back and forth as she cried. "I know it's hard, sweetie, but it's going to get better. You'll see. Everything's going to be all right."

Ciara cried and cried. It wasn't just because she had spent the whole summer so far wanting the wrong guy and hurting her friend, only to realize too late what it was that she actually wanted. For the first time since they announced they were going to split, Ciara was crying over her parents' divorce. Those tears had been bottled up for a long time, and she knew it was going to take a solid crying jag for her to get them all out.

"Don't worry," her dad said, as if reading her mind. "You can cry for as long as you need. I'm not going anywhere. I'm right here."

Chapter Nineteen

I'm sorry, sorry that I made you cry
Sorry, sorry that I told you lies

—*Stevie Wonder*

The lunch rush at the beach club café was in full swing, and sweat trickled down the back of Ciara's uniform shirt as she rushed around with glasses of club soda and plates of poached salmon with dill sauce, trying to keep her mind as much as possible on her job and as little as possible on the mess her life had become.

It wasn't working so well. Even as she took a table's order, her mind raced over the events from the past few days. Her parents had given her a deadline on a very important decision: she had until the weekend to decide whether she was going to move back to LA to live with her mom or stay in Santa Barbara with her dad, and even though she'd made up more than a dozen pro-and-con lists, Ciara still couldn't decide what to do. Maybe it would be easier to make that decision if her friends were talking to her, but Heidi was still giving her the cold shoulder, and it seemed like every time she called Kevin, he was hanging out with Marlene. Even when she phoned Em back in LA, she was so excited in the planning of Tim's upcoming surprise birthday party and how much she'd need her help to pull it off that Ciara hadn't even mentioned she was thinking of relocating seventy miles up the coast.

"I'm sorry," Ciara whispered to Heidi as she bustled past her carrying a tray of dirty dishes. She had taken to saying it just like that, under her breath, every time Heidi walked by. So far, it hadn't worked—Heidi was ignoring her more than ever—but Ciara figured maybe the repetition would eventually wear her down to the point where she'd be willing to talk. She wanted Heidi to forgive her. As much as the tortured chats about AJ had annoyed her throughout the summer, she realized she missed all the laughing and girlie confessions.

Sure enough, Heidi didn't turn around. Ciara took her next table's order and returned to the kitchen, where Heidi was just emerging with a tray of garden salads.

"Sorry!" Ciara said again, a little louder. Heidi tilted her chin in the air away from Ciara and picked up the pace, walking away as fast as her sneakers would carry her.

Ciara sighed and dropped off her order in the window leading to the kitchen.

"You girls having a fight or something?" It was John, the manager. He leaned with his elbow against the wall, his forehead wrinkled with concern.

"Yeah," Ciara said glumly. "It was my fault. I keep trying to tell her I'm sorry, but she won't listen. If you happen to see her, will you tell her I'm sorry too?"

John patted her shoulder comfortingly. "I sure will. Hope everything works out."

Ciara gave him a wan smile before rushing out to the cluster of tables again. She could hear someone over by the railing calling her. "Miss! Excuse me, miss!"

When she returned to the small indoor area, she saw that Heidi was deep in conversation with John, their heads bent close together at the kitchen window. John was gesturing animatedly with his fingers while Heidi bit her lip and nodded. Ciara's stomach tightened into a small tight ball of dread. She didn't want Heidi forgiving her because their boss had told her to. She wanted Heidi to want to forgive her as much as she wanted to be forgiven.

Heidi and John disengaged, and Heidi passed her on the way back out to the deck. "I'm sorry!" Ciara whispered again, this time more out of habit than any- thing else. To her surprise, Heidi's stony expression faltered for just a moment. Her lips spread a few millimeters wider than normal in what might have been the tiniest smile in the history of facial expressions. But it was a smile nonetheless. Ciara's heart soared. Was she finally getting closer to victory?

As the lunch rush slowed down and the crowd of diners on the deck gradually thinned, Ciara found she was getting more and more of a reaction from Heidi each time she whispered what had become her standard greeting. Heidi had gone from looking away from her to letting that tiny smile play over her lips longer and longer each time. Ciara sensed that she was near the breaking point.

She had an idea. She rushed into the kitchen, grabbed a piece of bread, and threw it in the toaster.

"Making yourself a snack?" asked Pablo, the head chef.

Ciara shook her head. "Something even more impor- tant," she said. When the toast was a golden brown, she found a can of bright yellow spray cheese and carefully wrote *sorry* in goopy orange script across the bread's surface. It wasn't the neatest print job ever, but she was sure that Heidi would have no trouble reading what it said. If this didn't work, she had no idea what would.

Heidi had taken a seat at one of the tables just inside the door and was stretching her legs by flexing and pointing her toes.

"I thought you might be hungry," Ciara said, putting a plate with the apologetic toast down in front of her.

"I'm not," Heidi said curtly. "So you can just . . ."

Her words trailed off as her eyes strayed to the writing on the toast. An odd little explosion seemed to happen behind her face—her skin was suddenly very pink and her chin began to shake, followed by her shoulders.

"Dammit, Ciara!" she finally said before exploding into laughter that bounced all over the room, out the door, and around the weathered wooden deck. She picked up the piece of toast, looked at it, and began to laugh again.

"Actually, I am kind of hungry," she said, biting into it. A small yellow blob of spray cheese settled into the corner of her lip, and she wiped it away with her finger before looking at Ciara. "Okay, I get it already. You wanna talk? Fine, let's talk."

She stood up and began heading to the door, Ciara following closely behind. They walked down the steps leading to the beach, and Ciara bent to remove her socks and sneakers, letting the warm sand scratch comfortingly at the bottoms of her feet. Now that she finally had Heidi's attention, would she even know what to say?

They got almost down to the surf line before turning to each other. "So . . . ," they began at the same time. They stopped, looked at each other, and laughed nervously. Heidi stared out at the flat blue horizon line of the ocean, and Ciara took a deep breath, ready to launch into her speech, even though she couldn't really remember it.

"So I'm really sorry about what I did," she began. "I had it all set up in my head that AJ would make the perfect boyfriend for me, and there was a lot of stuff going on in my life that made me think I needed a boyfriend."

"Did you, like, need stability because of your parents' divorce?" Heidi asked.

"Hmmm." Maybe Heidi had a point. Maybe she had been trying to re-create the kind of relationship her parents used to have. "I never thought about it that way, but yeah. Probably."

"I kind of figured it was something like that," Heidi said. "People get so weird when their parents get divorced. Kevin wouldn't come out of his room for like a month."

"I know, he told me," Ciara said. Just the thought of Kevin made her sigh a little on the inside. She couldn't believe it had taken her so long to realize just how amazing he actually was. And now it was too late.

"He's part of the reason I decided to talk to you

today," Heidi said. "I was hoping I could just go on not speaking to you until you went back to LA, but he conducted this whole campaign to get me to at least give you a chance to explain, and he kind of helped me see things from your point of view. Not that what you did is excusable, but he helped me understand why you might have done it anyway. He's a good guy."

"I know." This time the sigh was audible. She couldn't believe Kevin had secretly been talking to Heidi on her behalf. How sweet was that? "The greatest."

Heidi gave her a funny sideways glance, and her lips curled into a smile. "You like him, don't you?"

"No!" But Ciara felt the smile spreading to her own face as well. Heat rose in her cheeks. "Maybe."

"Yes . . . ," Heidi encouraged.

"Okay." Ciara blushed. "Yes. I like Kevin, okay? But it's too late. He's with Marlene now—and I am *not* snaking another girl's man."

Heidi sat down and picked up a handful of sand, letting it run slowly between her fingers. "You know, they're not really together," she said musingly. "I asked Marlene about it—they haven't even kissed. They've just been hanging out as friends."

"Really?" Ciara couldn't keep the hope out of her voice.

Heidi laughed. "Look at you, all excited over Kevin,

the hot single stud," she teased. The thrill at hearing that Kevin wasn't serious with Marlene mixed with hurt that he was spending so much time with her. All summer long, Ciara had felt like she and Kevin were "partners in crime." Now it seemed like he had that with Marlene instead of her, and the feeling of being replaced stung.

"Anyway," Heidi continued. "All I'm saying is, Kevin's more up for grabs than you probably think. If you want, I can help you figure out ways to get him."

"That's really sweet of you," Ciara said, turning to Heidi and smiling. "But I think I'm done with scheming for now. If anything's going to happen with me and Kevin, it'll happen because I just went with the flow. After all, look where plotting and planning got me with AJ . . . and with you."

"Yeah." Heidi sighed. "I would be a lot more pissed at you, but it's almost hard to blame you. There's just something about AJ that makes you go a little nuts. Like the way I started dressing like a rap groupie and going on about my wild side? That wasn't really me. I was just trying to get his attention. It's almost like, he's so hot and so sure of himself and what he likes, he can turn you into something you're not unless you're careful."

"I know exactly what you mean," Ciara said firmly.

"You know," Heidi mused, "he almost made us forget the cardinal rule: friends before mens."

"Bros before hos," Ciara added.

Heidi paused. "Mates before dates?"

They both laughed. "Speaking of dates," Ciara said. "What about the one you had the other night?"

"Oh, Sunday?" Heidi asked. She grinned at the memory. "It was awesome. *He* was awesome. We had a totally great time."

"Who was *he*, anyway?" Ciara asked.

Heidi looked down at the sand, biting her lower lip in a combination of embarrassment and glee.

"Remember that guy from Smoothie City?"

"Oh, Heidi!" Ciara shrieked. "The one with the tattoo? Not *him*!"

"Why not?" Heidi asked defensively. "He's a freshman at UC Santa Cruz majoring in biology, and he has three dogs! Guess what he wants to do after college?"

"Get another tattoo?"

"No, dumbass!" Heidi swatted her on the arm. "Go to veterinary school."

"That does sound kind of perfect for you," Ciara mused.

"We had an amazing time," Heidi said rapturously. "He knows someone who works at the aquarium, and we went there after hours and looked at all the fish and just talked and talked and talked. I mean, he's only working at Smoothie City as a summer job to make money for college. It's not like it's his career or anything."

"Whatever," Ciara said. "I'm glad you found someone who makes you happy, Heidi. That's seriously great."

"Me too," Heidi said, her eyes still shining. "Now you just need to get together with your perfect guy, and we'll be all set."

"I know," Ciara said, thinking of the look in Kevin's eyes when he had put his hand on her shoulder and told her everything was going to be okay. "But if it happens, it happens. If not . . . well, I guess I'll have to live with that."

Chapter Twenty

I don't wanna be a player no more
Now that I found the one I'm lookin' for
　　　　　　　　　　　　—DJ Kevlar

found it!" Ciara screamed. She quickly hit "print" on her laptop and waited for pages to start spewing out of the printer. Before the document had fully finished printing, she had grabbed up a handful of the papers and was running toward the kitchen, where her dad was marinating a chicken breast and watching the evening news.

"You found what, honey?" he asked.

"The answer," she said, waving the papers excitedly in front of his face. "What I want to do this fall."

"Well, then." Her dad chuckled. Even through his laugh, she could tell he was slightly nervous. "What is it?"

"Look at this."

"Hmmm." Her dad scanned the first page. "UC Santa Barbara Program for Academically Exceptional Youth. And what makes you think you're so academically exceptional, young lady?"

"Please." Ciara laughed. "Dean's list every semester at one of the top private schools in LA? Extracurricular activities and internships coming out my you-know-what? You know, I didn't spend all those hours studying in my room for my health."

"I know you didn't," her father said, putting his arm around her. "When it comes to ambition, you're your mother's girl."

"Look at the programs," Ciara said, pointing lower on the page.

"All right, all right." He read out loud: "Marine biology, advanced mathematics, music business . . ."

They looked at each other at the same time, and her dad smiled and nodded. "Bet I know which one you'll be going for."

"It's perfect," Ciara said. "And I already checked to make sure they partner with the local high school. You take regular classes at school in the morning, and then in the afternoon, you go to the college campus and take courses in your specialty. Do you have any idea how good this will look on my transcript?"

"You're aware that it involves staying here in Santa Barbara," her dad said. He was trying to sound serious, but she could see the smile threatening to burst onto his face.

"Um—duh?" Ciara said.

"Your mom's going to miss you. But I'll be happy to have you here."

"And I'll be happy to be here," Ciara said, throwing her arms around him and giving him a hug. "Plus, with these classes, I might be eligible for the accelerated graduation program."

"Okay," her dad said when they disengaged. "You need to do the right thing and call your mom and let her know what your plans are. You know she'll be disappointed and hurt, and you need to take responsibility for that. Sometimes you can't help hurting people in order to do what's right for you."

"Well, maybe I'll go down there and visit her before school starts," Ciara said. She wasn't looking forward to hearing the disappointment in her mom's voice, but maybe knowing they'd see each other soon would make it a little less harsh. Besides, it would be nice to go down to LA and see Em for a while.

She went to her room, closed the door, and sat at her

desk, staring at the screen of her cell phone before she got up the guts to call.

"Ciara!" Her mom seemed thrilled to hear from her and anxious all at the same time.

"Hi, Mom," Ciara said. Her voice sounded weak and timid in her own ears. "Listen, I wanted to apologize for the things I said to you when you were here."

There was a pause on the other end of the line. "It's okay," her mom finally said. "You had a right to be upset."

"Thanks, Mom," Ciara said. She pushed down the lump in her throat and went on. The hard part wasn't over.

"So have you made a decision about where you want to go to school yet?"

"Yes, I have," Ciara said. She took a deep breath. "There's a music business program for high school students through UC Santa Barbara, and I want to take advantage of it. So that means I'll be staying here."

"Oh." She could hear her mom trying to keep her voice calm, and she felt a twinge of guilt. Why couldn't she just make everyone happy all the time—even herself? "Well, I'm happy you found what you want to do. It's important to take opportunities like that as they come. But of course, I'll miss you."

"I'll miss you too," Ciara said, realizing she genuinely

meant it. "But I'll still see you—I mean, Santa Barbara and LA are only about an hour away. I'm going to come down before school starts and check out our new place down there, and I can come down on weekends sometimes and on holidays."

"Oh, good." Relief flooded her mother's voice. "It'll be so great to have you. I'll even make that Peruvian chicken from my mom's recipe. Remember how much you loved that as a kid?"

"Of course." A sudden fine mist rose in Ciara's eyes. She couldn't even remember the last time her mom had offered to make her favorite food—over the past few years, she had always been too busy with work and had left the cooking to her dad. Maybe the divorce would have some positive side effects after all. Maybe being away would make her mom appreciate her that much more when she was around. And maybe she would learn to appreciate her mom more as well.

"Great," her mom said. She sounded happy—as happy as Ciara felt. "So I'll see you next weekend?"

"I'll be there," Ciara assured her before saying "I love you" and hanging up. She was about to get up and tell her dad about the conversation when she had another thought: if she was going down to LA for the weekend, she should probably tell Em too.

She pressed her old best friend's speed-dial number

into her phone, expecting the call to go straight to voice mail the way it usually did when she called Em lately. But to her surprise, her friend picked up on the first ring.

"What's up, Ciara?" she asked.

"Hey, not much," Ciara said. She paused, realizing how ridiculous that sounded. All sorts of stuff was up.

"You're coming home soon, right?" Em asked. "We should start looking at classes and make sure we take some of the same ones."

"Actually . . . ," Ciara began. Her throat felt dry. Why did telling people about big decisions have to be so hard? "I'm staying in Santa Barbara this fall."

"You're kidding, right?"

"I'm not," Ciara said firmly. "I've made a lot of friends here, and there's this program at UCSB that I really want to take."

"Wow." Em sounded stunned. "I can't imagine Westwood without you."

"You'll still have Tim," Ciara pointed out.

"Sure, I know, but it's not the same as having you around," Em said. "So this is it—ta ta, it's been real, have a nice life?"

"No, I'm coming down next weekend to chill with my mom," Ciara assured her. "I promise we'll hang then."

"Next weekend? That's Tim's birthday—he'll be so psyched that you can come down! Oh, and you can help me set up and get the cake and run errands . . . will you? I mean, that way I can spend time with you without Tim around."

"Sounds great," Ciara said, smiling to herself. She would definitely miss Em, but she wasn't sorry to be leaving her Tim-centricity behind. "I'll give you a call before I come down, okay?"

"All right," Em said. "Oh, Tim's on the other line—gotta go."

At the beginning of the summer, Ciara would have been pissed at being blown off so quickly, but after what she'd been through, she could almost understand why Em was so crazy about her boyfriend. Not that she'd ever act the same way, she assured herself. When—er, make that *if*—Kevin was her boyfriend, she'd make tons of time for her girlfriends too.

She said good-bye and glanced around the room that was to be hers for the next year. Her gaze drifted toward the closet. It was time to pick out something to wear for the big night ahead.

*   *   *

"Wow, you know summer's almost over when the sun starts setting before eight," Ciara remarked as she, Heidi, and Todd of Smoothie City fame strolled through the quiet streets of downtown Santa Barbara to the club, which was all lit up like a jewel against the dim night sky.

"Oh, please don't talk about summer being over!" Heidi cried, wrapping her arms around Todd's waist and squeezing him tight. "That means my baby has to go back to school."

"Don't worry, sweetie," Todd said, nuzzling Heidi's hair. "You can come visit whenever you want, and I'll call and e-mail you every day. Promise."

Ciara smiled to herself. Normally, a couple as sickeningly sweet as Heidi and Todd would make her want to puke, but in the wake of the AJ debacle, Ciara was just glad her friend had found her perfect boy.

"I wonder if the boys are nervous right now," Heidi mused as they approached the entrance, following a stream of hip-hop fans in do-rags, knit caps, and tight Baby Phat jeans.

"Probably," Ciara said. "They've only been practicing for this gig all summer. It's more or less the biggest show they've ever played."

She thought that Kevin and AJ probably weren't the only ones feeling nervous right then. She hadn't seen Kevin in over a week, even though he'd sent her a few short, polite e-mails asking how things were going with Heidi. She wondered if everything would be different now that she realized how she felt about him. Would he know as soon as he saw her? Would she be able to tell if he felt the same way too? What if he didn't? What if he really was into Marlene, or still into Heidi, or had met some girl since she'd last seen him? Would the way she felt about Kevin turn into the same kind of embarrassing crush she'd had on AJ all summer?

She pushed the thoughts out of her mind as they waited in line to get their wristbands and be let into the venue. She was here to have fun, not mope over some guy. She'd done enough of that over the summer. Now she was just ready to watch her friends make some incredible music the way only the B-Dizzy Crew could.

"I can't believe how packed this place is!" Heidi said. The large, open dance floor in the club was filled to the point of bursting, the excited burble of voices almost drowning out the thud of A Tribe Called Quest over the speakers.

"This is great," Ciara said. "B-Dizzy's just the opening act, but if all these people are here already, it must mean their name is getting around."

"Look, there's Marlene," Heidi said, pointing all the way to the front. The room was so crowded that Marlene had actually gotten up on the lip of the stage to wave at them. "How are we going to get through all these people?"

"Follow me," Todd said. He took Heidi's hand, Heidi

grabbed Ciara's, and Todd began to lead them through the crowd, gently brushing past people as he politely excused himself. Unlike the dancers on the party boat, everyone at the club moved aside easily to let them pass. Before they knew it, they were standing at the foot of the stage, right next to Marlene.

"How did you do that?" Ciara asked admiringly.

Todd grinned. "Wait'll you get to college," he said. "You'll spend so much time pushing your way through crowded parties, it becomes second nature. The trick is just to be polite and firm."

"Welcome to the front of the room!" Marlene called, leaping off the stage and spreading her arms for a hug. Ciara noticed right away that there was something different about her. She'd ditched the plain black T-shirts she'd worn all summer and had on a filmy shell with a rose print, layered over a flesh-colored tank top and flowing gauchos. Her lips shimmered with gloss, and her eyes shone with an enthusiasm that Ciara hadn't seen in her all summer.

"You look great," Ciara said, wrapping her in a hug.

"Thanks," Marlene said. "I *feel* great."

"What happened?" Heidi asked. "You're like . . . all glowy and stuff."

Marlene just raised an eyebrow and smiled. "You'll see," she said mysteriously.

Ciara was about to start prying for details when the canned music faded out and the stage lights went up, bathing everything in an electric blue glow. The crowd shushed itself in anticipation, a final bark of laughter skipping over their heads like a flat stone on the surface of a lake and an embarrassed "shhh!" from the laugher's companion.

Kevin walked casually onto the stage, brought his fingers to his forehead, and tipped them toward the crowd in a small salute before positioning himself behind the turntables. His face looked strong and confident, and for once he wasn't wearing a visor, so she could really see how the haircut she'd made him get flattered his high cheekbones. Cheers filled the room, and Ciara's heart sped up like a thirty-three played on forty-five. She could hardly believe that Kevin had the same effect on her that AJ used to, but it wasn't just the usual quickening pulse, clammy palms, and tingling skin. It was something more. Seeing Kevin made her feel warm and safe inside, the way a cup of cocoa would make you feel after coming in out of the cold.

As cool and collected as Kevin looked, Ciara could tell he was nervous from the way the corner of his lip twitched. He flipped some switches on the mixer and dropped the needle onto the record. At that moment, AJ came leaping out from the sidelines and into the spotlight. The crowd went *nuts*, clapping and screaming until Ciara was surprised they had any voices left.

"Did you *see* that?" Heidi whispered as a tiny orange lace thong went flying onto the stage, landing at AJ's feet. AJ raised his eyebrows at the panties and shrugged comically.

Up there in the spotlight, AJ looked as beautiful as ever. For as long as she lived, Ciara would have to admit that he wasn't just hot—he was an amazingly, extraordinarily good-looking guy. That was part (not all, but *part*) of the reason the B-Dizzy Crew had been so successful with local audiences. It was why whenever he went somewhere, girls stopped and giggled and stared. It was why panties went flying onto the stage the moment he took the spotlight. But just because AJ was gorgeous, charismatic, and driven didn't mean he was the perfect guy for her. Nope—Ciara's perfect guy was behind the turntables, laying down some deeply complex scratching and loving the music instead of the glory. If only she had some way of knowing whether he felt the same way!

AJ launched into a song that had everyone dancing and waving their hands in the air. "Wow, baby," Ciara overheard Todd yelling in Heidi's ear, "You didn't tell me your friends were this *good*!"

Ciara grinned to herself as she bopped around to the beat. You'd have to be deaf not to realize that the B-Dizzy Crew was on fire.

After a couple more songs that practically had the walls shaking, AJ took a break, wiped his forehead with the back of his hand, and smiled down at the crowd as Kevin eased the beat down to a mellow background noise.

"You're an amazing crowd," AJ said, flashing his million-watt smile. "And I want to dedicate this next song to an amazing girl. She's the only one who can keep my ego in check—and after this show, believe me, I'm gonna need it!"

The crows laughed appreciatively as AJ's eyes scanned the crowd. "This one is called 'The Right Girl.' And it's for you, baby," he said, smiling tenderly.

Ciara's blood froze in her veins and her heartbeat slowed down so far she wondered if she was going comatose. AJ was looking *right at her*! This wasn't supposed to happen . . . he wasn't supposed to decide that they were right together after all . . . not when she'd finally come to the conclusion that Kevin was the perfect guy for her!

But to her surprise, AJ extended his hand down toward her—and past her. A small hand with blunt, pearly fingernails wrapped itself in his, and Ciara let out a long, ragged breath of relief as AJ pulled Marlene up onto the stage with him.

So *that* was why Marlene looked so radiant all of a sudden! After all their talk about how much sense it had made for them to break up, they were back together again. Even Ciara had to admit that Marlene would probably be good for him. She was the only girl who was straight up enough to call AJ on his ego and not fawn all over him like all the other girls and . . . well, and even like her. Ciara's cheeks flushed with embarrassment as she remembered all the times over the course of the summer that she'd gone out of her way to tell him how great it was that he had so much talent and drive. Sure, it was true and everything, but a guy as self-assured as AJ didn't need that kind of constant reaffirmation. Marlene would be able to boost him up when he needed it but also bring him down a peg or two when he got too into himself. As Ciara watched AJ rapping to Marlene on the stage and Marlene's happy smile, she realized they were perfect together.

At the end of the song, AJ kissed Marlene lightly on the lips and helped her down off the stage. Ciara could hear a chorus of disappointed sighs mixed in with the cheers. All over the room, AJ's female fans were realizing he was taken. Maybe a few of them were even formulating plans to get him anyway. Ciara laughed to herself. At least she had already learned her lesson about doing that—even if it did have to be the hard way.

"Sooooo," she and Heidi said at the same time, leaning close to Marlene.

Marlene's blush turned even more fiery red than before. "So what?" she said in mock defense. But she was smiling. "So it turned out I missed the lug head. Kevin helped me realize that and ran interference once I realized I wanted him back."

"Poor Kevin." Heidi sighed. "All he ever gets to be is AJ's best friend. I wonder when he'll get a girl of his own."

Hopefully before tonight is over, Ciara thought. But she kept it to herself.

*   *   *

At the end of their set, the B-Dizzy Crew did shout-outs. AJ thanked God, his mom, the Coup for letting them open, Tupac (RIP), Marlene, Kevin, and all his friends. Kevin thanked his parents, the Coup, AJ, his friends, and Qbert. A small thorn of disappointment lodged in Ciara's chest. Sure, she was one of Kevin's friends, but he hadn't thanked her specifically. Then again, why should he? She managed to keep a smile pasted on her face as the B-Dizzy Crew left the stage in a shower of thunderous applause and shouts of "encore!" But inside, she felt let down. She hadn't been able to admit it to herself, but ever since AJ had pulled Marlene up onstage, she'd been hoping Kevin would do something special like that for her too. She should have realized that pulling people up onstage and making a big public show of your love life was not at all Kevin's style.

"Encore, encore!" the crowd shouted. Someone began a chant of "One more song," and everyone joined in, stomping their feet, waving their hands in the air, and screaming rhythmically, "One more song! One more song!"

"Wow, I guess they were a hit," Heidi said, turning to Ciara and Marlene.

"Jeez, listen to them," Marlene agreed. "I guess so."

Finally, AJ came loping back onstage, followed by Kevin. The air swelled with hoots and cheers, and AJ held up his hands for silence.

"Okay, all right already." He laughed, taking the mike. "You want one more song, we'll give you one more song. Just chill already."

"Yaaaaaaaaaaaaaaaaaay!" screamed the crowd.

"DJ Kev-lar?" AJ said, sweeping a hand toward Kevin. "Why don't you take it away?"

"All right." A hush fell over the room as Kevin leaned into the microphone. It was clear that he wasn't used to speaking to crowds. "This one's for Ciara, if she's out there."

With that he ducked his head, put on a record, and

dropped the needle. The opening beats of "Still Not a Player" came floating through the speakers. Ciara's head began to spin as the vocals kicked in. Not only had Kevin just dedicated a song to her, but it was *her* song—the song that had changed the way she thought about boys, about relationships, about *everything*. How did he know?

And then she remembered that foggy morning at the diner on the dock, the morning after they had almost kissed. She had played that song on the jukebox and said she'd been into it lately. And he had remembered!

Kevin was scratching the record, remixing it before the crowd's astonished eyes, as AJ rapped over it. He'd ditched the Big Pun lyrics and written some of his own, and they sounded even better than the original. The crowd was dancing so hard she could feel the floor shake. And in the midst of all of this, Kevin looked down off the stage, right into her eyes, and smiled.

When the song was over, he didn't even bother going backstage. He came right down to the lip of the stage, where she and Heidi and Marlene and Todd were standing, and leaped off. The lights in the house had come up, and the air was full of crosscurrents of conversation, shrill bites of laughter, and the dull thud of the canned music they played between sets. But Ciara didn't hear any of it. The only thing in her universe that moment was Kevin leaping off the stage and coming toward her.

It was only a matter of inches, and in seconds he was standing right in front of her, his forehead gleaming with sweat from the stage lights and a shy, expectant smile on his face.

To Ciara, he was the most perfect boy in the world right then. He looked down at her, his grin stretching expectantly from cheek to cheek. Her heart sped up past forty-five to seventy-eight and she felt as dizzy, happy, and excited as she had ever been.

"Did you like the song?" Kevin asked, blushing a little.

All of a sudden, the truth came crashing into Ciara's mind. Kevin had liked her all along. Looking into his eyes, she knew it all made sense . . . the time he spent helping with Project Woo-ha, despite never getting results.

There was only one answer to his question. Ciara leaned forward, put her hands on his shoulders, and kissed him. When they pulled away, Kevin smiled down at her, his hands still firm and warm on her shoulders. For the first time that summer, Ciara felt like she'd gotten everything she wanted.

"Of course I liked the song," Ciara said. "Did you like the kiss?"

Kevin grinned. "Woo-ha," he said.

*Ever wish your dream boy could be your real-life boy? Here's
an excerpt from Hailey Abbott's*

Waking Up to Boys

All thoughts flew out of her mind as Chelsea stared at Todd, unable to think of what to say. Those slightly crooked, strangely bright white teeth. That messy, I-live-on-the-water look to his light brown hair. The strong shoulders and arms. Oh yes, and that telltale smirk. It was Todd, all right. He hadn't changed a bit. But Chelsea had. She was his height now. And being able to see straight into his lake-blue eyes was suddenly extremely distracting.

Chelsea blushed at the awkward silence. She knew she had it bad.

"Earth to Chels," Todd was saying, waving his hand in front of her face. "Swallow too much lake water?"

Chelsea found herself laughing harder than she had

when Justin Timberlake hosted *Saturday Night Live.*

"Long time no see," he said, coming toward her with his arms outstretched.

"Hey, man, I'm all wet," she said, laughing again nervously and shrinking back. She was sure that the last thing Todd wanted was a big water stain on the front of his faded hunter-green Abercrombie tee.

"I can see that," Todd smirked. "How's the water?"

"Brilliant, as always," Chelsea replied, trying not to let her eyes linger on him too long. It was weird feeling this nervous around him. She'd always liked him, but he used to be so easy to be around.

"You looked pretty decent out there," Todd said, kicking at a splinter in the dock.

"Thanks. I didn't realize you'd seen me practicing." Warmth flooded her chest at the compliment. Todd was notoriously tough, saving his praise only for when it was really deserved. "I've been snowboarding my butt off all winter."

"Well, it shows," Todd assured her. "But the ending was a little wobbly on that last jump."

The critique was so typically Todd. "Think you could have done better?" she asked, narrowing her eyes at him.

"Is that a challenge?" He grinned. "Because you're not the only one who's been boarding her ass off all winter, you know. They could barely scrape me off the half-pipe back in Utah once all the snow melted."

"We'll see how you do on your first run," Chelsea retorted.

"Yeah?" Todd patted the large duffel bag hanging off his shoulder. "I've got a wet suit right here if you want to put your money where your mouth is."

"I'm already wearing mine," Chelsea pointed out. She watched as Todd's eyes traveled down the length of her body, and she suddenly wished she hadn't said anything. There was no doubt that the suit molded to all the wrong parts of her long, lean frame, making her legs look scrawny and her boobs totally flat.

"Then I'll be right back," he said, slinging the duffel bag higher on his shoulder and heading toward the lakeside bathhouse. "And then let's get out on the water and you can show me what you've got."

As she waited for him to emerge, Chelsea couldn't tell if her heady, eager feeling of adrenaline was from the thought of another run behind the boat or from seeing Todd again. Of course, if it weren't for Todd, she might never have picked up wakeboarding in the first place. She'd been all about the skiing—on water and snow—until the hot new wakeboard instructor showed up at Glitterlake the summer she was fourteen and made her think that having both feet strapped into a single board might not be the worst idea after all—especially if he were there to make sure she stayed upright, his broad golden hands guiding her firmly as he barked instructions into her ear over the motor's roar. She honestly hadn't counted on falling so deeply in love with the sport itself . . . or on being so good at it. Before long she was trying jumps and grips that even Todd had trouble with. And even though he had never come right out and said it, Chelsea was pretty sure that tough, competitive Todd wasn't wild about being upstaged by a girl.

"I can't wait to hit this lake," Todd said, swaggering out of the bathhouse in his wet suit. Even though it came down to his ankles and zipped all the way up his neck, Chelsea's knees went weaker than after she'd landed her first 360. The suit's stretchy material clung to his body, hugging his chest and broad shoulders.

Todd hopped gracefully into the boat and extended his hand to help Chelsea off the dock. Normally there was no way she would let a guy think she needed his help to do *anything*, but the chance to touch Todd was too tempting. She rested her palm in his and felt the strength in his arm as he escorted her onto the gently bobbing craft.

As Todd leaned over to untie the rope from its slip, Chelsea slid into the driver's seat and started up the motor, feeling the boat sputter to life underneath her.

"So how was your winter?" Todd asked as she drove them out onto the water. "Do anything fun besides board your butt off?"

Chelsea gulped inwardly. The truth was, she hadn't—in between spending every afternoon on the slopes and helping her parents out around the resort, she didn't have much of a life. But there was no way she was going to let Todd know that. "There's nothing more fun than boarding," she challenged instead.

Todd's sky-blue eyes crinkled up at the corners when he laughed. "I concur," he said. "That's basically all I did too. But, unlike you, I didn't have that pesky little thing called school interrupting me."

"I'm so jealous," Chelsea sighed. Sitting in a classroom all day felt like torture when she could see the snowy peaks of Sierra Mountain sparkling in the distance. "School shouldn't be in the daytime. All that light goes to waste. I could make much better use of it out on the water."

"Well, someday you too could become a professional board bum," Todd joked, reaching out and pushing playfully at her shoulder. The contact made her insides turn to syrup, and a thought suddenly occurred to her. Was Todd . . . could he be . . . flirting with her? Was he teasing her because he could tell that she liked him? Or was it something more? Chelsea wondered if by some miracle he was starting to see her as someone in his league—someone more than just a wakeboarding student. Was it possible that Todd could think of her as a *girl* . . . like, the kind of girl he could flirt with?

Chelsea slowed down as they reached the middle of the lake and let Todd climb out behind the boat. Even with his face half-covered in goggles, he was still the single hottest guy she had ever seen. "Well, feast your eyes on this," he said before sliding into the water, sending all her hopes and dreams about his seeing her as more than just the competition swirling down the drain.

Oh, I will, Chelsea thought, amused by how true his words really were.

She sped up the boat, watching the long, white wake stretch out behind in the many rearview mirrors positioned to give the driver the optimal view of the rider behind. She was so used to the way he moved—they'd been practicing together for years, and she'd memorized the way his body worked.

She watched as Todd gathered momentum, swinging his body from side to side. She could tell from the way he was riding nearly fifteen feet outside of the wake that he was planning a big jump. Coming back into the wake, Todd stood up tall on his board and flipped suddenly into a double back roll, turning all the way upside down in the air. Chelsea winced as she realized he was underrotating, giving the towrope too much slack so that he didn't get enough of the natural speed of the boat. She sped up slightly, hoping to make the rope taut enough for him to land the trick successfully, but it was too late. Without the natural momentum of the boat's speed, Todd couldn't get all the way around. He skidded to a halt on his butt several feet outside the wake. Even over the motor's roar, Chelsea could hear him cursing.

She slowed down long enough for him to regain his footing and then took off again, watching his body language grow bolder and his moves more confident. She could tell he was going to try the double back roll again—and this time he was going to nail it. Sure enough, Todd's body flew through the air in a set of perfect cartwheels, his strong legs flexed high over his head. He landed expertly and flashed Chelsea a triumphant smile before using the towrope to pull himself back toward the boat.

"Well, how was it?" he asked, climbing into the boat and shaking the water droplets out of his hair.

"You looked great!" She decided not to mention the butt skid—even though she knew *he* would have mentioned it if their roles had been reversed.

"Man, it's good to be back here. I missed this place." Todd stretched his arms over his head so that his soaked wet suit settled into the crevices between his hip and stomach muscles. He let his arms swing back to his sides and smiled down at her. "You ready to let me drive for a while?"

Chelsea stood up to give him the driver's seat. As she did, the boat rocked below them and Todd automatically reached out to steady her. She drew closer to him, her heart pounding as the boat's rocking gently subsided. Todd's face was so close to hers that she could count the drops of lake water on his eyelashes. They stood that way in silence for a moment until he abruptly let go and slid into the driver's seat.

"Let's see what you can do," he said, casually resting an elbow on the wheel.

Chelsea smirked. "Oh, I'll bring it," she said, looking straight into his eyes.

Her heart still hammering, she slipped her feet into the bindings of her board and strapped it on nice and tight before sliding out into the water. Even though her body was tired from riding less than an hour before, she was determined to show him just how much she'd improved over the winter. After a few grabs, she felt confident enough to try a roll of her own. Taking a deep breath and heading way outside the wake, Chelsea launched herself into what had to be the most perfect double back roll in the history of wakeboarding. She landed well wide of the wake, her knees and feet rock-steady beneath her. She was about to do a little happy dance when she caught a glimpse of Todd's frowning face in the rearview mirror. Chelsea's triumphant smile faltered and then disappeared. Was he upset that she'd landed the same trick he'd just messed up on, and on her first try? She suddenly felt the effort of the day's two practice sessions seeping through her tired muscles. She signaled him to slow down and dragged herself back into the boat. She sank into the passenger's seat and unclipped her bindings. Todd's forehead was still lined with a scowl, and his shoulders hunched over the wheel.

"Nice job out there," he said, looking straight ahead. She could feel the tension.

"Thanks," she replied, her heart sinking at the dreaded note of envy in his voice. She *knew* she'd looked great on the water. And she also knew that that just might be the problem.

Read these juicy summer page-turners!

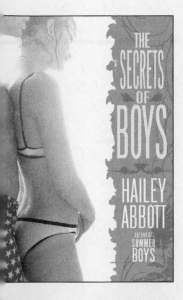

The Secrets of Boys

A California girl like Cassidy Jones should be out on the beach, not stuck in summer school! But her life heats up when she meets the worldly and romantic Zach— she can't stop thinking about him, even though she already has a boyfriend. Cassidy wishes her pal Joe was around to help her figure out the secrets of boys, but he's hundreds of miles away. Will she be able to ignore her feelings for Zach—or will temptation be too strong to resist?

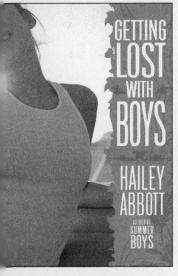

Getting Lost with Boys

Cordelia Packer hates the unexpected, but she's in for a surprise when Jacob Stein offers to be her travel companion, all the way from San Diego to her sister's place in Northern California. Before she knows it, her neatly laid out summer plan has turned into a wild road trip, where anything can—and does—happen. Who knew getting lost with a boy could be so much fun?